DON'T CALL ME
HERO

ALSO BY RAY VILLAREAL

Alamo Wars

My Father, the Angel of Death

Who's Buried in the Garden?

DON'T CALL ME HERO

Ray Villareal

PIÑATA
BOOKS

PIÑATA BOOKS
ARTE PÚBLICO PRESS
HOUSTON, TEXAS

Don't Call Me Hero is made possible through a grant from the City of Houston through the Houston Arts Alliance.

Piñata Books are full of surprises!

Arte Público Press
University of Houston
452 Cullen Performance Hall
Houston, Texas 77204-2004

Cover design by Mora Des!gn

Villareal, Ray
    Don't Call Me Hero / by Ray Villareal
    p. cm.
    Summary: Ninth-grader Rawly Sanchez's life is hard—his brother is in prison, he works at his mother's restaurant to help make ends meet, he is failing algebra and the girl he has a crush on does not know he exists—but when his dramatic and impulsive rescue of a wealthy celebrity from a flooded creek makes him famous, he does not know what to think about his new-found popularity.
    ISBN 978-1-55885-711-7 (alk. paper)
    [1. Conduct of life—Fiction. 2. Fame—Fiction. 3. Middle schools—Fiction. 4. Schools—Fiction. 5. Mexican Americans—Fiction.] I.
PZ7.V718Do 2011
[Fic]—dc23

                                                    2011025927
                                                         CIP

Printed in the United States of America
October 2011–November 2011
United Graphics, Inc., Mattoon, IL
12 11 10 9 8 7 6 5 4 3 2 1

For my daughter, Ana

CHAPTER ONE

Rawly Sánchez sat in a booth at the back of his mother's restaurant and stared blankly at his math sheet. He had gotten a 64 in algebra on his last report card, and it looked like he was headed toward another failing grade.

"How do you expect to run a restaurant if you can't do math?" his mother had scolded him. "I have to figure out paychecks, taxes. I've got to keep up with the inventory. I run the register and total up customers' checks. I need to know math to do all that."

Rawly knew math. At least as much as his mother did. He could add, subtract, multiply and divide without too much trouble. He even had a decent understanding of fractions and percentages. But the homework his teacher, Mr. Mondragón, had given him didn't make any sense.

Write an algebraic equation for each of the following and solve, it said at the top of his paper.

Rawly read the first problem again.

1. An airplane pilot is flying from Atlanta to Seattle at a speed of 525 miles per hour. When the plane is 660 miles from Seattle, the pilot is informed that he won't be cleared to land for 90 minutes. At what constant speed should the plane fly to arrive in 90 minutes?

Rawly sighed. To him, the problem was as impossible to understand as the hieroglyphic writings of the ancient Egyptians he had learned about in social studies class. It had taken the discovery of the Rosetta Stone to help decipher the meanings of those strange drawings. Rawly felt he would need some type of Rosetta Stone to help him figure out his homework.

He moved on to the next problem. That one didn't make any sense, either. Neither did the third or fourth one.

Mr. Mondragón had recommended that Rawly start attending Saturday morning tutoring class. But if Rawly did that, he wouldn't be able to see Jaime any more.

Almost every Saturday, for the past eleven months, Rawly and his mother had gone to visit his brother in Midway, Texas. Now, after tomorrow, it would be Thanksgiving break, at the earliest, before he would get to see Jaime again.

Rawly looked at his watch. Nine fifty-two, it said. In eight minutes his mother would close the restaurant, and he could put another wasted Friday night behind him.

Suddenly the doors swung open. Cruz Vega and five of his teammates walk in. With them were Cruz's newest girlfriend, Sharon Gilroy, and four other girls.

The North Oak Cliff Bisons had just won their sixth straight game, having defeated their long-time rivals, the Ernie L. Fedette Falcons, 31 to 7. Cruz had thrown two touchdowns in the game and had scrambled into the end zone for another. The playoffs were on the horizon, there was no question about it. But the Bisons had never doubted they would make the playoffs. Their goal since the beginning of the school year had been nothing short of winning the Class 5-A State Championship. And Cruz

Vega knew better than anyone that he was the Bisons' ticket for getting them there.

Standing under the archway at the entrance of the dining room, Cruz snapped his fingers. "Service! We need some service here!"

His group laughed.

The only customers in the restaurant were an elderly couple that had arrived a half hour earlier. The couple glared at the rowdy teenagers. The man said something to the woman that made her nod in agreement.

Sharon Gilroy looked around the restaurant and wrinkled her nose. The plaster walls were a dingy, off-white color. Pictures of a Mayan village had been amateurishly painted on them. A large pyramid, the famed Temple of Kukulcán, stood in the center of the village. Strands of fat, Christmas tree bulbs were strung across the low ceiling, adding color to the dimly-lit room. Mariachi music played from the speakers above the cash register.

Sharon wrapped an arm around her boyfriend's waist and said, "Come on, Cruz, let's get out of this dump. Anyway, I think the restaurant's closed."

He shrugged her off. "No, it ain't. Somebody'll be here in a second." He looked around for someone to seat them. "Maybe La Chichen-Itza ain't anything fancy schmancy, but at least they serve real Mexican food here. Not like in those uppity, over-priced restaurants like the Mexi Cali Diner that use words like guac and chimmis because guacamole and chimichangas sound too ethnic. Nah, this place is just fine."

Other than Sharon Gilroy, no one else in the group had questioned Cruz's restaurant choice at which to celebrate their win. After all, he was the hero of the game.

"Service!" Cruz snapped his fingers again. "Hey! Anybody working here tonight?"

Rawly ignored him. He was not about to get up to greet Cruz and his friends. They could seat themselves, for all he cared. Or better yet, they could just leave.

Cruz Vega, superstar quarterback. Big donkey deal.

Rawly knew him from school. Not that they were friends or anything. Cruz was a senior and a hotshot football jock, who didn't have time to waste on lowly freshmen like Rawly. Cruz was also a celebrity of sorts. His name was often featured in the football game results in *The Dallas Morning News*.

```
Vega, Bisons, Too Much for Lakeview
Quarterback Vega Throws Three TD Passes in Win
Bison Quarterback Cruz Vega's Late TD Keeps
North Oak Cliff Unbeaten
```

A pep rally had been held earlier in the day in the school auditorium, and the entire student body was invited to attend. Cruz spent most of his time onstage blabbing about himself, shooting his mouth off about his "destiny." What especially irritated Rawly was that he had to listen to Cruz repeat his stupid catchphrase over and over: "We're on Cru-u-u-z control, baby! Woo!" He must have said it a dozen times.

Rawly wondered about the blond glued to Cruz's side. He had never seen her before. It didn't matter. There would probably be a different girl with Cruz the next time he saw him.

"Hello-o-o?" Cruz called. "We've got some hungry customers here. If somebody doesn't show up pretty soon, we're leaving."

Good, Rawly thought.

At that moment, Rawly's mother stepped out of the kitchen. When she saw the teenagers, she grabbed an armload of menus and hurried up to them. *"Buenas noches.* How many in your party?"

"How many in our party?" Cruz turned to his friends. "You hear that, guys? I told you we were having a party."

His friends clapped and cheered.

The old couple looked up again and gave them dirty looks.

"There are eleven of us, ma'am," Cruz said. "Unless you count him twice," he added, pointing to Juan Salinas, a monster-size, defensive tackle, affectionately known as Big Feo. "Then we've got an even dozen."

Big Feo grunted.

"Give me just a minute and I'll get a table ready for you." Mrs. Sánchez rushed to the back of the restaurant and told Rawly to help her push four tables together.

Rawly cursed under his breath. Why did those clowns have to show up now? He flung his pencil at his math sheet and dragged himself out of the booth.

After Cruz's group was seated, Rawly served them glasses of water, baskets of tortilla chips and cups of hot sauce.

Cruz clapped him on the back. "Thanks, Pancho. Tell you what. You give us real good service, and I'll leave you a dollar. Okay?" He flashed Rawly a quick wink.

"I'm not your waiter," Rawly said coldly. "And my name's not Pancho. It's Rawly."

"Raleigh?" Cruz snickered. "You mean Raleigh as in the capital of Virginia?"

Raleigh's the capital of North Carolina, you moron, Rawly wanted to say, but he held his tongue.

"Hey, you guys hear what this kid's name is?" Cruz said. "It's Raleigh, as in Raleigh, Virginia."

"Hi, Virginia," Sharon Gilroy said sweetly with a wiggle of her fingers.

"Hey, Virginia, bring us some tortillas," Big Feo said. "And some more hot sauce."

Rawly scowled at him. "Somebody will take your order in a minute."

"Well, tell them to hurry it up," Cruz said. "We're starving."

As Rawly walked away, Cruz tossed a half-eaten tortilla chip at him. "C'mon, Pancho, move it!"

Rawly's face burned with anger. He wished he could turn around and slap that smug smile off Cruz Vega's face.

Jaime would have done it. He'd punch Cruz's nose so far into his face, it would stick out on the other side of his head, like a unicorn's horn. Jaime could whip all those loud mouths. But then, none of those guys would have ever spoken to Jaime the way they did to him. They wouldn't dare.

Teresita and Isabel, the only servers working the nightshift, waited on Cruz and his friends.

Rawly returned to his booth, but he could still hear the group talking and laughing. It was impossible not to.

" . . . burned their secondary . . . ran in that third touchdown like their defense had fallen asleep . . . made a fool out of their so-called strong safeties." Cruz couldn't get his fill of bragging about himself. "We're gonna go all the way to the state championship. And you wanna know why? 'Cause we're on . . . "

"Cru-u-u-z control, baby! Woo!" the group chimed in.

The guys high-fived each other. Sharon Gilroy snuggled up to Cruz and kissed his neck. The old couple rose from their table, paid their bill and left. But not before complaining to Rawly's mother about the noisy teenagers.

It was almost eleven o'clock, and the restaurant had closed, but the partying continued. Not that Rawly's mother minded. Sure, it was late, and the kids were loud. But they were bringing in money, something La Chichen-Itza desperately needed.

Rawly craned his neck and stared at the group as they ate and joked and laughed. A strange feeling tugged at him. He wanted to get up to join the party, to be part of their celebration.

Rawly eyed the blond as she continued to caress and kiss Cruz. He tried to imagine what it would be like to have her as his girlfriend—to feel her body pressed against his, to taste the tenderness of her lips, to enjoy the sweet scent of her perfume.

Cruz turned around to find someone to refill his iced tea glass and caught Rawly staring at them. He smiled and winked.

Rawly shrank against his booth, red-faced.

The partying continued until almost midnight. Finally the group paid and left.

As they made their way to the parking lot, Rawly stood at the front window and watched them. The guys and girls exchanged handshakes and hugs. Sharon Gilroy gave Cruz a long kiss before slipping into the car with him.

After they drove off, Rawly remained at the window, transfixed. He wondered where they might be going next. Home, probably, but maybe not. When Jaime was a senior in high school, he used to stay out late—long past midnight—with his friends.

"*Ándale*, Rawly. Don't just stand there," his mother said, snapping him out of his trance. "Let's get this place cleaned up so we can go home."

Rawly looked around the room. Teresita and Isabel were flipping the chairs upside down and sitting them on the tops of the tables so the floor could be swept and mopped.

"Some day all this will be yours," his mother often told him. "Yours and Jaime's." She said it as if the restaurant was supposed to be some great inheritance Rawly and his brother should look forward to owning.

Rawly couldn't imagine spending the rest of his life working seven days a week, running the restaurant. Jaime certainly wasn't going to do it, especially not after his accident.

Rawly had no idea what his future held for him, but one thing he knew for certain—he was not going to be stuck in this crummy restaurant forever.

While he swept, Rawly's mind drifted off to another place, to another world. Where he was idolized. Where the girls swarmed around him. Where people were dying to be his friend.

Where he was Cruz Vega.

CHAPTER TWO

The next morning, Rawly drew open the living room curtains and stared out the window. Rain poured down in thick, silvery sheets. Gray clouds huddled together, and flickers of lightning illuminated them. Thunder reverberated with each flash of light.

Rawly dreaded the thought of having to make the trip to Midway on the wet highway. Riding in the rain always made him skittish. It stirred memories of the night of Jaime's accident.

If only Jaime had listened to their mother. She had pleaded with him not to leave the party.

"Don't be rude to your guests," she told him. "They came to help celebrate your graduation."

But Jaime didn't want to spend graduation night at La Chichen-Itza with a bunch of uncles and aunts he hardly knew. He had other plans, big plans, for his celebration, and they didn't involve a bunch of boring relatives.

Jaime's best friend and fellow graduate, Aaron Camacho, had called three times, wondering what the hold up was. "Hurry up, *vato*. We're waiting for you."

"Don't be out too late," Mrs. Sánchez told her son when she realized it was useless to try to make him stay.

"I won't," Jaime promised. He planted a kiss on her cheek. "But don't stay up for me. I've got my key. I'll let myself in when I get home."

It would be weeks before Jaime set foot in their house again.

Rawly waited in the kitchen while his mother checked to make sure the doors were locked. He leafed through a comic book, one of a dozen he was taking to his brother. Jaime was almost twenty-two, but he still enjoyed reading comic books—*X-Men* and *Spider-Man* being among his favorites.

After graduation, Jaime had planned to enroll in art classes at one of the junior colleges. His goal was to work for Marvel Comics or DC some day.

His mother was against his decision. She wanted him to go to a four-year college— to the University of Texas or Texas Tech—to study business, with the hope that one day, he would take over the restaurant. But after his accident, both those dreams were shattered.

The rain grew stronger as soon as Rawly and his mother pulled onto Interstate 45. It pelted the windshield with fierce, watery bullets. Traffic slowed to a crawl after they passed Corsicana. A blue Chevy Silverado had plowed into the back of a green Honda Civic when the driver of the Honda swerved out of his lane to avoid hitting a dog that had scampered onto the highway. The accident backed up traffic for miles, and it didn't seem as if it was going to clear up anytime soon.

Finally, at a quarter after eleven, Rawly's mother exited the interstate and followed a nine-mile stretch of woods and fields to the town of Madisonville. Herds of horses and cattle, grazing on both sides of the two-lane blacktop, stared stupidly at them as they drove by. Past Madisonville, a white water tower welcomed them to the connecting town of Midway, Texas, population 333.

As they traveled along the winding, asphalt road, Rawly's mother said, "I don't want you asking Jaime any questions about the night of his accident. I want this to be a pleasant visit. You understand?"

"But I didn't ask him," Rawly said. "Jaime's the one who started talking about it the last time we came."

"Well, don't . . . " His mother paused. "Just don't bring it up, all right?"

"I won't," Rawly said. He looked up at the sky. It had stopped raining. The sun even teased an appearance, but it quickly retreated behind a cloud.

They turned into the parking lot of a long, rectangular, red brick building and got out of the car. Rawly read the sign in front.

FERGUSON UNIT

TEXAS DEPARTMENT OF CORRECTIONS

CHAPTER THREE

The Ferguson State Prison Farm stands authoritatively in a large open field. Two metal perimeter fences with four rows of spiraling razor wire surround the structure. Six guardhouses are stationed around it. A chapel with a long white cross and a tall white steeple faces the street.

A guard met Rawly and his mother in the parking lot and inspected their car.

Once they were given clearance, they proceeded to the gate house, where they were met by two other guards. One of the guards had them empty their pockets. The other one told them to stand with their arms outstretched. He waved a metal detector wand up and down the sides of their bodies. Rawly and his mother had long overcome any fear or indignities they may have felt at being searched. It was something they tolerated on a regular basis.

"You can't take those in," the guard with the metal detector wand told Rawly when he saw the comic books in his hand.

"But they're for my brother."

"Sorry. You'll have to take them back to the car, or you can leave them here until you finish your visit."

Rawly looked at his mother. She shook her head. Reluctantly, he handed the comic books to the guard.

They were issued passes to the contact room. They walked down a sidewalk until they reached a beige building. Rawly's mother knocked on the steel door and a guard let them in.

White plastic tables were spaced throughout the contact room. Inmates sat at the tables, visiting with friends and family.

Three guards paced around the room. They wore gray uniforms with navy-blue baseball caps. A Texas Department of Criminal Justice patch was sewn on one shirt-sleeve, and an American flag was stitched on the other. A blue stripe ran down the sides of their pants.

The contact room offered no privacy.

Jaime sat next to an inmate who was visiting with his wife and three kids. Like all other prisoners, Jaime wore white scrubs and black boots. His dark-brown hair, which he had always worn over his ears when he was in high school, was now closely cropped. His ears stuck out from the sides of his head like butterfly wings. His right arm bore a tattoo of a snake crawling out of a skull's eye socket. On Jaime's left arm was a large drawing of Wolverine, one of the X-Men, posed in a lunging position, with his metal clawed hands extended in front. Cyclops, the Beast and Nightcrawler filled the rest of his arm.

Jaime rose and greeted his family.

"I tried to bring you some comic books, but a guard took them away from me," Rawly told his brother.

"Yeah, they don't let you bring anything in here," Jaime said. "You know that. But thanks anyway for trying."

Rawly knew he couldn't bring the comic books inside the prison. The rules had been explained to him when he first tried to bring them in eleven months ago. Rawly was hoping that maybe after almost a year of visiting his brother, the guards would cut him some slack, but no such luck.

"You do that yourself?" Rawly asked, when he saw the snake and skull tattoo on Jaime's arm.

Jaime gazed at his most recent body art. "I drew the picture, but Martín helped tattoo it." Martín Gómez was Jaime's cellmate.

Mrs. Sánchez looked away. She did not approve of Jaime's tattoos.

When Jaime was thirteen, he got his first tattoo—a small J and S on his left hand between his thumb and forefinger. His mother exploded with anger when she discovered it and accused him of trying to look like a gang member. The tiny J and S were now lost among the much larger and more graphic drawings on Jaime's arms and body.

"How's the restaurant doing?" Jaime asked. "Business getting any better?"

His mother smiled uncomfortably. "It . . . It's doing real good," she lied. "You should've seen it last night. It was packed." She bumped Rawly's knee under the table. "Wasn't it, Rawly? Wasn't it real busy last night?"

Taking his cue, Rawly bobbed his head. "Yeah, uh, we had a full house. In fact, the last group of customers, a big party of eleven, didn't leave until almost midnight."

Rawly felt he needed to support his mother's story, because he had let it slip out during their last visit that the restaurant was doing poorly.

"That's good. How about you, 'manito? Anything new?"

"Not a whole lot," Rawly said. "My friend Nevin Steinberg and I are going to the fair in a couple of weeks."

"Nevin Steinberg?" Jaime laughed. "Isn't he that goofy kid you said you couldn't stand?"

Rawly shrugged. "Nevin's okay most of the time. He's gotten better since middle school."

"I hope so," Jaime said doubtfully. He pulled a folded sheet of paper from his shirt pocket. "Check this out, 'manito. I've started working on a comic book character."

On the lined notebook paper was a drawing of a masked superhero, dressed in dark-gray tights with black boots and gloves, speeding through a city street. A tornado was pictured on his chest. "This is El Torbellino. He can run super fast. He's like a Latino version of the Flash," Jaime explained.

"That's tight, man," Rawly said, admiring his brother's art.

"Keep it. It's yours," Jaime said. "I don't have a story yet, but I've got a bunch of ideas. Maybe when you come back next time, I'll have a storyboard to show you."

Rawly whipped his head around and stared at his mother.

She sighed and said, "Go ahead. Tell him."

Rawly lowered his eyes and swallowed hard. "Jaime, I'm not going to be able to see you for a while."

Jaime's face grew somber. "Why not?"

Rawly glanced at the inmate sitting with his family across them. They were joking and laughing, as if they were at a church picnic instead of in the contact room at the Ferguson State Prison Farm. "Because I flunked algebra," he muttered. "Now I have to start going to tutoring classes on Saturdays."

Jaime frowned. "Yeah? For how long?"

Still refusing to meet his brother's eyes, Rawly said, "I guess until my grades get better."

"What's your problem, man?" Jaime said loudly.

One of the guards walking by stopped and stared at him. Jaime waved and mouthed the word *sorry* to indicate that he wasn't causing trouble.

"Don't you listen in class?" Jaime's tone softened, but it was still serious.

"Yeah, but algebra's hard," Rawly said.

"So what? If things are hard, you work harder, that's all." Jaime glimpsed around the contact room. "Look at these guys, *'manito*. They're a bunch of losers. Things got hard for them, so they gave up and tried to take the easy way out. Do you want to end up like them? Like me? A loser?"

Rawly finally looked up at his brother. "Jaime, you're not a loser. You're better than any of these guys in here."

"Yeah? Well, there's a dead woman's family who'll tell you a different story," Jaime said bitterly.

Mrs. Sánchez kicked Rawly under the table. "I told you not to bring up Jaime's accident," she whispered through clenched teeth.

"But I didn't," Rawly whispered back.

There was an awkward silence.

The conversation picked up again, but nothing more was said about the accident or about the dead woman.

When their visit was over, Jaime hugged his brother. "I want you to bring up those grades, you hear? I don't want you failing. Make me proud of you, *'manito*."

"I'll try," Rawly promised.

CHAPTER FOUR

Nevin Steinberg walked up to a J.C. Penney store clerk who was folding sweaters and tapped her on the shoulder. "Excuse me, ma'am. May I talk to you?"

The clerk, an old, unnaturally thin woman peered down at him from above the rim of her glasses. "May I help you find something?" Her voice was high and sounded more irritable than helpful.

"Um . . . no." Nevin licked his lips and glanced around the store. "This may not be anything, but, um, do you see that kid over there?" He pointed at Rawly, who was standing on an aisle near the women's lingerie section. "This is probably none of my business," Nevin said, "but I've been watching him for a while, and well, you see, my dad works security at Dillard's, and he's taught me to look out for certain things."

The clerk removed her glasses and fixed a frigid stare on Rawly. "What's the matter? Did you see him shoplift something?"

"No. No. I don't think he's stealing stuff," Nevin said. He lowered his voice. "It's just that . . . It's kind of embarrassing, ma'am, but . . . "

"What is it?" the clerk asked with an edge of impatience creeping into her voice.

Nevin cleared his throat. "Well, whenever that kid thinks no one's looking, he slips ladies' underwear over his head, like a mask. I've seen him do it twice already." He looked back at Rawly. "I thought I should tell someone what I saw."

The clerk gaped at Rawly, pop-eyed. Her gaunt face grew pinched with disgust. She sat an orange sweater on the table and marched down the aisle.

"Young man!" she spat out. "May I help you?"

Rawly turned and smiled. "No, thanks. I'm waiting for a friend."

"Is that right? And where is your . . . *friend?*"

Rawly, who had not immediately noticed her accusatory tone, looked around the store.

Nevin hid behind a dress rack and watched with glee.

"He's around here somewhere."

The clerk noticed Rawly's empty hands. "Are you buying anything?"

"No, but my friend . . . "

"Then perhaps you need to leave!" She aimed a twig of a finger in the direction of the store's exit.

Rawly's eyes widened. "Why? What'd I do?"

Nevin pressed his hand against his mouth, trying to keep a laugh from exploding.

"Do you think no one saw you?" the clerk fumed. "Shame on you!"

"But I didn't do anything," Rawly protested.

"Please leave!"

"But my friend . . . "

"Do I need to call security?"

Rawly didn't answer. With the clerk's venomous stare bearing down on him, he skulked out of the J.C. Penney store, dumbfounded.

Nevin caught up with him in the mall a few seconds later. "Dude, where were you? I've been looking all over the store for you."

Still reeling from what had just happened, Rawly croaked, "I got kicked out of Penney's."

Nevin's jaw dropped. "You did? Why?"

"I don't know." Rawly's eyes were glassy. "I was just minding my own business, waiting for you, when this lady came up and started yelling at me."

"Really? What did she say?" Nevin asked, sounding shocked.

"She said someone saw me doing something and that I should be ashamed of myself," Rawly said.

"Yeah?" Nevin's eyes started to water as he tried to hold in his laughter. "Maybe she thought you were doing something weird."

"Weird? Like what?"

"Oh, I don't know. Maybe she thought you were putting ladies' underwear on your head."

"Why would she . . . ?"

Nevin burst out laughing.

"Doggone it, Nevin!" Rawly gave him a hard shove. "Why do you do stupid stuff like that?"

Nevin wiped the tears that had leaked out of his eyes. "Aw, chill out, dude. What's the matter? Can't you take a joke?"

"That wasn't funny," Rawly said. "That old lady probably thinks I'm some kind of freako."

"*She's* a freako," Nevin retorted. "She looks like she ought to be standing in a cornfield scaring away crows."

"I'm leaving." Rawly wheeled around and headed toward the mall's exit.

Nevin caught up to him and hung an arm on Rawly's shoulders. "Hey, don't be sore. Come on, dude, I was just messing with you. Look, I'm sorry, okay?" He bit his lower lip to suppress another laugh that was trying to erupt.

Nevin was surprised the clerk had bought his story. He thought she'd see through him and realize that he and Rawly were together, and that he was playing a practical joke on his friend. But as he'd heard his father, the public relations director at the Dallas Zoo, say a million times, "It's all about the sell. It's not what you say but how you say it."

"Tell you what, dude. Let's go to the food court. I'll buy. Besides, it's pouring out there. You don't want to wait for the bus in the rain, do you?"

It was barely misting.

Rawly shrugged off Nevin's arm. "I don't need you to buy me anything."

"Please?" Nevin coaxed. "They've got a Sonic here. I'll buy you a nice, delicious, banana split. M-m-m." He ran his tongue across his lips. "How about it? A banana split with lots of whipped cream and a cherry on top."

Rawly peeked at his watch. It was ten after five. He still had a little time before he had to go to work. "All right, but I'll buy my own banana split."

At the food court, Rawly recognized a couple of guys from his school, sitting at a table, eating McDonald's burgers, but he didn't know their names. He nodded his chin at them and they nodded their chins back in acknowledgement.

Standing in the Sonic line, Nevin said, "Listen, Rawls, as long as you're buying yourself a banana split, um, can you buy me one, too? I just remembered. I don't have any money."

Rawly glared at him. "You're too much, man. You know that?"

Nevin laughed. "Better to be too much than not enough, dude. Right?"

Rawly checked his wallet. He had a five and three ones. He hated having to buy two banana splits, but he really wanted one, and he couldn't eat a banana split while Nevin sat there watching him, salivating like a hungry dog.

Luckily tomorrow was payday. Rawly would then have enough money to buy ten banana splits if he wanted.

While they ate their treats, Nevin asked, "So which suit do you think I ought to buy? The black one, the gray one or the navy one with the white pinstripes?"

Rawly shrugged. "Either one's fine, I guess. A suit's a suit." He scraped the last bit of melted ice cream with his spoon and ate it. He resisted the urge to pick up the plastic dish to lick it clean. Not long ago, he would have done it without hesitation. But now that he was in the ninth grade, he thought it was uncool to do that sort of thing —in public, anyway.

"Come on, dude, that's not an answer," Nevin said. "You told me you'd help me pick out a suit."

Rawly wiped his mouth and dropped his paper napkin into his empty banana split dish. "Okay, if I were you, I'd go with the black one. Black's good for any occasion —including weddings. Didn't your mom make any suggestions as to what you should buy?"

Nevin snorted. "Are you kidding? If it was up to her, she'd have me dressed up in short pants, knee-high socks and a bowtie."

Rawly nodded. He had been around Nevin's mom long enough to know that there was some truth to what he said. "I'm surprised she's letting you choose your own suit. I mean, for something as important as your sister's wedding."

Nevin raised his plastic dish to his mouth and swiped his tongue across it. He immediately sat it back down when he saw Rawly staring at him. "Yeah, well, ever since my Bar Mitzvah, she's been trying to teach me to be more responsible. You know, now that I'm a . . . *man.*" Nevin stressed the word "man" like a bleating sheep. "By the way, you *are* going to Miriam's wedding, aren't you?"

"I'll try," Rawly said. "But algebra tutoring classes start this Saturday."

Nevin slapped his head. *"Oy, vey!* How'd you get stuck with having to go to algebra tutoring?"

"Easy," Rawly said. "By stinking at algebra. The worst part about it is that I won't be able to visit my brother any more."

"Oh, yeah. How's Jaime doing these days?"

"About what you could expect, given his circumstances," Rawly said. He tapped his nose with his finger, and then pointed to Nevin.

Nevin picked up his napkin and wiped chocolate syrup from his nose. "I don't get it, dude," he said. "What is it about algebra that you don't understand?" Nevin had participated in the Math Olympiad competitions every year since the fourth grade, and he couldn't imagine why math would be difficult for anyone.

Rawly folded his arms on the table and shook his head. "It's the word problems that kill me, man. I just don't get them."

"There's nothing to them," Nevin said. "If you know how to read. You *do* know how to read, don't you?"

Rawly quirked his mouth. "Of course I do."

"That's right," Nevin said. "You're the comic book king."

"There's nothing wrong with reading comics," Rawly said indignantly.

"No, there isn't," Nevin agreed. "So if you can read comic books, you can do word problems."

"How do you figure that?" Rawly asked, thinking that Nevin was setting him up for one of his jokes.

Nevin leaned back in his chair and crossed his legs. He slipped his red plastic spoon in the corner of his mouth and clenched it between his teeth, like a pipe. "Let Professor Steinberg give you a crash course on how to solve word problems." Nevin inhaled with the spoon in his mouth. Then he took out the spoon, held it between two fingers, pursed his lips, and pretended to blow out smoke. "Okay, let's say that the Joker's caught Batman in his Joker Destructo Deathtrap Device."

"There's no such thing in the comics," Rawly said.

"Don't complicate things, dude. The point is, Batman's trapped, see? And he has to find a solution to his predicament." Nevin took another puff from his imaginary pipe. "Now, Batman's going to escape from the Joker's Destructo Deathtrap Device. We know that, right? 'Cause if he doesn't, DC can't sell any more Batman comics. Anyway, Batman goes over all his options. He thinks of everything he knows about deathtraps 'cause he's been in plenty of them in all his years of being Batman. He makes a few calculations in his mind and . . . bingo! He figures out a solution to his problem. He escapes from the Joker's Destructo Deathtrap Device and captures the Joker. End of story. At least until the next issue." Nevin put the spoon back in his mouth, crossed his arms and smiled with satisfaction.

Rawly gave him a puzzled look. "I don't get it. What does that have to do with algebra?"

"Everything, dude." Nevin sat up. "Next time you go to algebra class, think like Batman. You're in a predicament. You've got a problem to solve. Go over all your options. Consider everything you know about algebra, and you'll come up with an answer."

Rawly smiled and said, "You know, Nevin, sometimes you almost make sense."

"Sure, I do. And if you'd listen to me more often . . . " Nevin glanced to his right and saw two girls approaching them. He leaned into Rawly and whispered, "Chick alert at three o'clock."

Rawly turned as Iris Solís and another girl neared their table.

Nevin stood. He pretended to remove a hat and bowed. "Good evening, *señoritas*. Would you do us the honor of joining us at our humble table?"

Iris said, "Nevin Steinberg, Rawly Sánchez, this is my cousin, Miyoko Elena Chávez."

Nevin bowed again. "A pleasure to meet you, *señorita*."

Miyoko threw back her long, jet-black hair and greeted them.

Rawly had seen Miyoko at school, but since they didn't share classes, he had never spoken to her. He had often wanted to talk to Miyoko, but he always chickened out. He usually did when it came to meeting pretty girls.

"Sientay, sientay, por favor," Nevin said, mangling the little Spanish he knew. He pulled out two chairs.

Rawly's heart leaped when Iris's gorgeous cousin sat next to him. "Mi-yo-ko," he said. "Sounds Japanese."

"It is," Miyoko said. "My mom's Japanese."

"Really?" Nevin said. "My mom's Sofatshese."

"Sofatshese?" Miyoko asked. "What's that?"

"You know, my mama's *so fat she's* been declared the fifty-first state."

The girls laughed. Rawly, who had long lost his appreciation for Nevin's sense of humor, rolled his eyes.

"My name means 'beautiful generation child,'" Miyoko explained. "At least, that's what my mom told me."

Nevin patted her hand and winked. "Mama definitely knew what she was doing when she gave you that name."

Miyoko blushed.

"What are you girls doing here?" Rawly asked, wanting to get in the conversation.

Iris pushed aside a banana split dish and sat a small Hot Topic bag on the table. "Just hangin'. You?"

Nevin quickly interjected, "Rawly brought me to see a scalp doctor. I have a terrible rash on my head. Listen." He pretended to scratch his head. With his other hand, he scraped his fingernails on the bottom of the table, making a loud, grating sound. "My scalp feels like sandpaper."

Miyoko laughed. "You're funny."

"It runs in the family," Nevin said. "My grandma's part hyena." He made laughing hyena sounds.

Miyoko laughed again.

Rawly loved the sound of her voice. And the way her half-moon eyes sparkled when she laughed!

"We were on our way to Ghouls & More to check out the Halloween costumes," Miyoko said. "You guys want to join us?"

Rawly wished he could accept her invitation. He'd love to get to know the "beautiful generation child" better, but he had to decline. "Sorry," he said. "I have to work tonight. My mom owns a restaurant, and I have to help out."

"Really?" Iris sounded impressed. "Which one?"

"La Chichen-Itza on West Jefferson," Rawly said.

"La Chichen-Itzaaa, cha-cha-cha," Nevin sang and danced in his chair. "Specializing in chicken pizzaaa, cha-cha-cha."

Rawly looked at the time. It was almost five-thirty. He promised his mom he'd be at the restaurant by six. He rose from his chair. "Sorry, but we've got to go."

Nevin frowned. "Dude, are you kidding? We've just been offered an invitation to party with two charming and lovely *señoritas.*" He wrapped his arms around the girls. "You go ahead. I think I'll stay for a while."

Rawly couldn't believe it. Nevin had asked him—begged him—to come to the mall to help him pick out a suit for his sister's wedding. Rawly had even bought him a banana split. Now Nevin was abandoning him. Worse, he was going to spend the evening with Iris and Miyoko while he had to work all night cleaning tables.

Rawly excused himself. As he made his way out of the food court, Nevin mocked in a singsong voice, "See ya. Wouldn't wanna be ya!"

CHAPTER FIVE

On Monday morning, Rawly was on his way to the cafeteria when Nevin suddenly darted past him. Travis McHenry and three other guys were chasing him.

"I'm gonna getcha, Steinberg!" Travis hollered.

For a second, Rawly considered joining Nevin in case he needed help, but the thought vanished as quickly as it came. Rawly was no hero. He had never even been in a fight. Travis and his gang would make dead meat out of him if he tried to butt in. Anyway, he figured Nevin would get out of whatever trouble he had gotten himself into. He always did.

Rawly spotted Miyoko and Iris standing in front of a bulletin board near the main office. His heart fluttered. He walked up and said, "Hi, Miyoko, remember me?"

She gave him a blank look. Then she smiled and said, "Oh, hi. Sure, you're Nevin's friend from the mall the other night."

Nevin's friend.

She didn't know his name. Rawly wished she had answered with something like, "Of course I remember you. You're Rawly Sánchez, the cute guy I met at the mall, who was sitting at the food court with that silly, immature kid."

"This is Rawly," Iris reminded her.

"Actually, my name's Rolando," Rawly said. "When I was little, my parents used to call me Rollie for short. But when I got to school, I spelled Rollie the way it sounded to me—R-A-W-L-Y. Anyway, the name stuck, so now I'm Rawly."

Miyoko listened with indifference.

Rawly wanted to say something clever, something funny, that would make her laugh the way Nevin had done, but nothing came to mind. No jokes, no witty remarks. The next words out of his mouth were, "What are you girls doing standing here? Aren't you going to lunch?"

Man, that is so lame. I sound like a hall monitor accusing them of not being where they're supposed to be.

Miyoko pointed to the bulletin board. "We were reading the flyer for Open Mic Nite. We're thinking about trying out for it."

"Really? Do you have any talent?" Rawly asked.

Oh, brother, what a stupid thing to say. Of course she has talent. Otherwise, why would she be considering auditioning for Open Mic Nite?

"I play the guitar," Miyoko said. "And I sing a little."

"I bet you're good," Rawly said.

Miyoko flipped her hand in a side-to-side motion. *"Más o menos."*

"I play the clarinet," Iris said. "I'm in the band, you know."

Rawly ignored her. Mustering up his nerve, he told Miyoko, "I was on my way to lunch. Want to join me?"

"Sure," Iris answered right away.

"You go ahead," Miyoko said. "I need to talk to Mr. Mondragón about something."

You're the one I was inviting, Rawly thought. *I don't want to eat lunch with Iris Solís.*

At that moment, Nevin appeared from around the corner and stopped in front of them, gasping for air.

"What happened?" Rawly asked. "Why were those guys after you?"

Nevin took a couple of deep breaths. "Dude . . . some people . . . just don't have . . . a sense of humor. All I did was ask Travis McHenry to smell my elbow. It wasn't my fault he ran his nose into it."

"Hi, Nevin," Miyoko said.

He bowed. *"Hola, señorita. ¿Cómo estar?"*

"It's *cómo estás,"* Rawly corrected him.

Miyoko's face lit up. "Nevin, have you seen this?" She pointed to the Open Mic Nite flyer. "You should try out for it. I think you'd be great onstage. Maybe you could do a comedy routine or something."

Nevin acted surprised. "A comedy routine? Why? Do you think I'm funny?"

"I think you're hilarious," Miyoko said. "The kids will eat it up."

Nevin's face grew serious. He looked down and shook his head. "I can't."

"Why not?" Miyoko asked.

"I . . . I'd rather not talk about it." Nevin's face crumpled

"Nevin? Is something wrong?" Miyoko asked with concern.

Nevin cupped his hands over his face. "I went to see the doctor yesterday, and . . . and . . . " He sniffled.

Miyoko gasped. "Nevin, what is it?"

Rawly remained skeptical. Miyoko had just met Nevin, but he'd known him for a while. He had a feeling Nevin was setting her up.

"The doctor told me . . . " Nevin's lower lip quivered. "He told me . . . "

"What, Nevin?" Miyoko's eyes grew misty. "What did the doctor tell you?"

"He said I have a growth . . . " Nevin gulped. " . . . outside my brain."

"What?"

"It's true!" Nevin began to bawl. "He called it a . . . a . . . c-c-cranium!"

"Oh, no!"

A confused expression filled Iris's face. "Wait a minute. We all have craniums."

Nevin stopped crying. "We do?"

"It's the part of the skull that encloses the brain." Iris looked at Rawly. "Isn't it?"

"So there's nothing wrong with me?" A false sense of relief washed over Nevin.

Rawly rolled his eyes.

Nevin threw his hands up in the air and bounced up and down. "Glory, halleluiah! I'm all right! I'm all right!"

Miyoko playfully swatted his arm. "Oh, Nevin, you had me so scared."

"Aw, don't pay any attention to me. I was only serious."

"You mean you were only . . . " Miyoko stopped. "See? That's what I'm talking about. You'll steal the show."

"How about you, Rawly?" Iris asked. "Do you have some hidden talent we don't know about?"

"He sure does," Nevin said. "Rawly's a magician. He can make good grades disappear just like that," Nevin added with a snap of his fingers. "And this Saturday, he's going to start attending algebra tutoring class to learn part two of the magic trick. How to bring those good grades back."

"You too?" Miyoko said glumly. "That's why I was on my way to see Mr. Mondragón. He's making me go to Saturday tutoring."

"Really?" Rawly said with a lilt in his voice.

Algebra tutoring just became a lot more pleasant.

Nevin wrapped an arm around Miyoko and escorted her down the hallway. "No need to see the Dragon Man, my dear. Professor Steinberg will personally tutor you on the fine art of mathematics. By the way, do you read Batman comics?"

Iris turned to Rawly. "You going to lunch?"

"Yeah, I suppose," he said with a sigh.

They followed Nevin and Miyoko to the cafeteria.

CHAPTER SIX

After school, Rawly and Nevin got off the DART bus at the intersection of Zang and West Jefferson and headed for Heroes & Villains, a comic book store that specialized in graphic novels and collectible action figures. Sometimes they stopped there on their way to La Chichen-Itza. The restaurant was located two blocks down, past the old Texas Theater, where President Kennedy's alleged assassin, Lee Harvey Oswald, had been captured.

Life-size statues of Superman and Batman stood like guards at the entrance of Heroes & Villains. In the middle left side of the store, just below the ceiling, a Spider-Man figure clung to the wall. He was shooting his webbing at a Green Goblin figure, stationed on the opposite end.

A glass case at the front of the store housed a variety of collectible statues and busts of comic book figures—the Incredible Hulk, Doctor Doom, the Submariner, Captain America and the Mighty Thor on the top shelf—Superman, Wonder Woman, Aquaman, Green Lantern, Lex Luthor and the Joker on the bottom. Less expensive plastic action figures stood on shelves or hung on metal racks in each aisle.

Cardboard boxes, filled with thousands of old comic books, sat on tables, which were situated in a maze-like fashion throughout the store. The newer issues were lined in magazine racks along the walls. Graphic novels, including manga, were shelved in bookcases.

Sid Lundy, the owner of Heroes & Villains, greeted the boys when they walked in. He wore a blue T-shirt with a picture of Captain America's shield on the front. A pair of black suspenders, decorated with tiny Batman insignias, held up his brown trousers.

"The Dallas Comic Con's taking place in a couple of weeks," Sid announced, handing the boys a flyer promoting the event. "Kenny O'Brien's going to be there. So are Jack Corrigan, Tim Soo and Alexi Malenkov." Sid's eyes crinkled mirthfully. "And guess who's going to lead a panel discussion?" Without waiting for an answer, he blurted out, "Johnny Romita Junior! Can you believe it? Jazzy Johnny Romita himself!" Sid folded his arms on the counter and smiled.

"Wow, Sid!" Nevin replied with delight. "Really? You're right. I can't believe it. When did you say the event's taking place?"

Sid picked up another flyer from the counter and pointed at it. "October twenty-fifth and twenty-sixth. Tickets are only fifteen dollars."

"That's fantastic, dude," Nevin said. "Thanks for letting us know. I can hardly wait."

When they walked away, Nevin whispered to Rawly, "Who are all those guys Sid was talking about? And what the heck is The Dallas Comic Con?"

Rawly made a face to show he disapproved of the way Nevin had led Sid on. "They're comic book artists. The Dallas Comic Con's a comic book convention where fans get to meet famous comic book writers and illustrators. Tons of movie celebrities usually show up, too."

"Yeah? Like who?"

Rawly glanced at his flyer. "It says here that Thomas Hayden Church is going to be signing autographs on the twenty-sixth."

"Should that name ring a bell?" Nevin asked. Comic books had never captured his interest. The only times he went inside Heroes & Villains was with Rawly. He did like the monster toys the store sold, though. Nevin had acquired a sizable collection of horror action figures, much to his mother's disapproval. She often complained to her husband about Nevin's "obsession" with the macabre.

"Thomas Hayden Church is the guy who played Sandman in *Spider-Man 3*," Rawly explained. "And it says here that Linda Blair's making an appearance, too."

"Oh, I know who she is," Nevin said. "She's the chick from *The Exorcist* with the spinning head and the pea-soup vomit."

Rawly smiled and nodded.

"So who's this Johnny Comida guy that Sid was salivating over?" Nevin asked.

"It's not Comida. It's Romita," Rawly said.

"Well, I'm thinking *comida* 'cause I'm starving." Nevin patted his stomach. "When are we going to eat?"

"In a little bit," Rawly said. "Johnny Romita Junior and his father, Johnny Romita Senior are legends in Marvel Comics. Come here. I want to show you something." Rawly led Nevin to a bookshelf and pulled out a copy of *Essential Spider-Man Volume 2*. "Johnny Romita Senior was the second artist to draw Spider-Man, after Steve Ditko left the company." Rawly flipped open the book and thumbed through it. "Romita Senior took over the series with issue thirty-nine. That's where the Green Goblin discovered that Peter Parker was really Spider-Man. Romita is also the one who finally revealed what Mary Jane Watson looked like." Rawly turned the pages. "See? Here she is. 'Face it, Tiger. You just hit the jackpot!'" he read. "Johnny Romita Junior also worked on *Spider-Man,* as well as *Daredevil, X-Men,* and *Thor.*"

Rawly talked comics the way other guys discussed sports or movies or TV shows. He could rattle off millions of bits of trivia about them. Nevin tried to listen patiently, but his mind wandered as Rawly prattled on.

"Jack Kirby . . . blah, blah, blah . . . Marvel Universe . . . blah, blah, blah . . . New Avengers . . . blah, blah, blah . . . Dr. Strange . . . blah, blah, blah . . . and this is the Civil War series where Congress passed the Superhuman Registration Act that forced superheroes to unmask. And over here—"

"Whoa, dude. Slow down," Nevin cried. He clapped his hands over his head. "My brain's on fire. It can't absorb all that knowledge at one time."

"Sorry." Rawly placed the book back on the shelf. "I was just trying to give you a little background information on some of the characters."

Nevin wobbled his head in an exaggerated manner. "Background information I can handle, but you're trying to cram a whole college course on comic book history into my head."

Rawly faked a smile. It was a waste of time trying to explain comic books to Nevin. He didn't have any appreciation for them. Most of the guys at school didn't, either. Sure, they'd all seen the superhero movies and had watched the cartoons on TV, but did any of them know the mythology behind the characters? Would any of them know who Rawly was talking about if he mentioned the names Jerry Siegel and Joe Shuster? The only people Rawly felt comfortable discussing comic books with were Jaime and Sid Lundy. Jaime was the one who had introduced him to Heroes & Villains.

Rawly walked down the next aisle to see if the latest issue of *Teen Titans* had arrived. While he looked for it, Nevin picked up an action figure of The Thing from the Fantastic Four and one of the She Hulk. He pressed their faces together as if they were kissing.

"Hey, dude, what kind of babies do you think The Thing and this green chick would make if they got married?"

Rawly pretended not to hear. He searched the magazine racks but didn't find what he was looking for. He picked up an issue of *The Flash* and thumbed through it. He thought about Jaime's superhero, El Torbellino. It would be cool if Jaime could write and illustrate the story and get his comic book published. Maybe Sid could carry copies of it in his store.

Nevin placed the action figures back on the shelf. His eyes were drawn to a comic book cover that featured a female Asian warrior named Yui Tanaka. He picked up the comic book and flipped through it. Then he held it in front of Rawly's face. "Hey, dude, do you think this chick looks like Miyoko Elena?"

Rawly stepped back to get a better look. The girl in the comic book had long black hair that hung in waves down her back. She was dressed in a red halter top with a matching bikini bottom. Black boots rose up her legs and stopped just above her knees. A gold band was wrapped around her head. She was swinging a long-handled Japan-

ese samurai sword at orange and black creatures that
looked like giant grasshoppers.

"Yeah, a little," Rawly said, smiling. "She's kind of
hot."

Nevin blinked with surprise. "Whoa, dude. Did you
just say Miyoko was hot?"

Rawly caught himself. He could feel his face turning
red. "No, man, I said the girl in the comic book was hot.
I didn't even mention Miyoko's name."

"Yeah, but you also agreed that this chick looks like
Miyoko," Nevin said. "So if you think the chick is hot,
then what you're also saying is that you think Miyoko's
hot, too." Nevin stared at the girl in the comic book. "Not
that I disagree with you, dude. I think Miyoko's pretty
hot myself."

What was Nevin saying? That he liked Miyoko? Was he
going to try to make a move on her? Rawly had seen him
flirting with her, of course, but that didn't mean anything.
Nevin flirted with all the girls. Rawly hoped Nevin wasn't
serious about Miyoko. If he was, then Rawly didn't stand
a chance with her. Nevin had him beat by miles in the
charm department.

"I'm going to check out the monsters," Nevin said. He
slapped the comic book against Rawly's chest. "Here, I'll
let you and Miyoko spend some alone time together."

Rawly studied the cover art. Yui Tanaka did resemble
Miyoko Elena. He decided to buy the comic book, but not
today. He would come back another time by himself. For
now, he settled on a copy of *Green Arrow*.

While he skimmed through it, Nevin returned. He
had an Iron Man toy sitting on the back of a plastic model
of Doctor Octopus. He hopped them across a shelf, with

Iron Man riding Doctor Octopus like a rodeo bronco-buster.

"Hey, Rawls, if I was a superhero, do you know what kind of power I'd like to have?" Nevin sat Doctor Octopus and Iron Man on a magazine rack. "You think I'm going to say something like super strength or the ability to climb walls, right?"

Rawly turned away. He was trying to concentrate on his comic book.

"We'll, you're wrong, dude," Nevin said. "If I had a choice of super powers, I'd like to have the power of forgetfulness."

Rawly looked up from his comic book with a smirk on his face. "That's not a power. Lots of old people have it. It's called Alzheimer's." He nudged Nevin away from the magazine rack. "Watch where you're standing, man. You're going to tear the comics."

Nevin straightened. "No, dude, this is how my power would work. Let's take this morning, for example, when Travis and those other morons were chasing me. If I had the power of forgetfulness, I'd zap them with it, and they'd immediately forget why they were after me. Pretty cool, huh?"

Rawly didn't answer. He was used to tuning Nevin out whenever he started babbling about nothing. Rawly continued reading his magazine.

"Or, let's say a couple of bad guys are robbing a bank," Nevin went on. "I could zap them with my forgetful ray, and they wouldn't remember what they were doing. The police could nab them easily and haul their butts off to jail." Nevin bunched his fists on his hips and puffed out his chest. "I'd call myself . . . " He deepened his voice like a radio announcer's. "Amnesia Man!"

Rawly decided to buy *The Flash* and the *Green Arrow* comics. He checked his wallet. He had thirty-four dollars left from the money his mother had paid him for cleaning tables. He looked around to see if there was anything else he wanted. He picked up a copy of *Green Lantern*, glimpsed at the cover and realized he already had that issue. Rawly decided not to buy anything else. He and Nevin were planning to go to the state fair, so he thought he'd better save his money for that.

"Dude, I just had a thought," Nevin said. "What if we did a skit about Amnesia Man for Open Mic Nite? You and me. I'll be Amnesia Man and you can play my sidekick . . . Airhead."

Rawly sighed. "I've told you a thousand times, Nevin. I am not interested in taking part in Open Mic Nite. I don't like performing in front of other people." He wrinkled his face. "Airhead? Why Airhead?"

"'Cause. If you were Amnesia Man's sidekick, you'd constantly be exposed to his forgetful ray, so your mind would always be blank. You'd be an airhead."

"Forget it," Rawly said and made his way to the checkout counter. He stopped at the glass case to admire the plaster action figures. He wished he could afford them, but they were too expensive, with prices starting at sixty dollars for the smaller models. The large statue of Superman ran for almost three hundred bucks. Rawly figured he'd have to win the lottery to be able to afford that one.

Nevin leaned against the glass case. He quickly straightened when he realized what he was doing. He didn't want to get yelled at again. "Hey, Rawls, if you could be a superhero, what kind of powers would you want to have? But you can't say forgetfulness. I already have dibs on that one."

Rawly didn't respond, sure that Nevin would make fun of whatever answer he gave.

Nevin gazed at the Superman statue. "You'd want to be like Superman, right? Super strength. The ability to fly. And X-ray vision! Woo hoo! You could have all kinds of fun with that power."

Rawly tried to give him a stern look, but he cracked up as Nevin, with a goofy grin, wiggled his eyebrows.

"Get your mind out of the gutter, man," Rawly teased.

Rawly *had* fantasized about being a superhero. Millions of times. In his dreams, he could fly. He had huge muscles. He possessed incredible strength. And everybody loved him, especially the girls.

Usually in his dreams, the girls' faces were unrecognizable. Recently, though, one of them had come into focus. It was unmistakably Miyoko Elena's. She always had her arms wrapped around him, touching his muscles, wanting to kiss him.

Rawly looked up at the Spider-Man figure. He had never found it believable that Peter Parker remained a nerd after he gained his super powers. If Rawly had written *Spider-Man*, Peter Parker would have beaten the snot out of Flash Thompson and anyone else who tried to pick on him.

The people at Marvel Comics had a saying about Spider-Man: *With great power comes great responsibility.* What they should have added was: *With great power comes great confidence.*

If Rawly was a superhero, he wouldn't need to be clever or charming, like Nevin Steinberg. He wouldn't need to be a star football player on a championship team, like Cruz Vega. Being a superhero would bring him all the attention he could ever want. People would be dying to get their picture taken with him. They'd beg for his autograph. He'd be front-page news. And the girls . . .

"Hey, dude, when are we going to eat?" Nevin asked, snapping Rawly back into reality. "I'm starving." He squeezed the folds of his stomach, like a mouth, and whined in a high voice, "Feed me! Feed me!"

They made their way to the counter where Rawly handed Sid Lundy the comics and a twenty-dollar bill.

While Nevin waited, he picked up an action figure of Captain Marvel and marched him across the counter. "Hey, Rawls, do you think superheroes are braver than ordinary people?"

"Sure. That's what makes them superheroes."

"Well, now, I wouldn't exactly say that," Sid interjected. "There are lots of ordinary folks who risk their lives every day. Police officers, firefighters and soldiers, for example. They're our real heroes." He rang up Rawly's purchases and slipped the comic books into a black plastic bag with the Heroes & Villains gold-colored logo on the outside.

"Yeah, but Nevin was asking about superheroes," Rawly said, feeling a little embarrassed that Sid had corrected him. "I think their super powers make them more confident. It gives them the courage to do things other people would be too scared to try."

"Maybe," Sid said. "But there are lots of superheroes without powers—Batman, the Phantom, and Green Arrow to name a few. Still, they always manage to get the job done."

"So what makes a hero a hero, Sid?" Nevin asked.

"Oh, courage, sacrificing oneself for the good of others, being able to overcome adversity," Sid mused. "I think that's a pretty good start."

Nevin nodded.

Rawly stuck his Dallas Comic Con flyer inside his bag. "Thanks, Sid."

"You bet." He came around the counter and walked the boys to the door. "Tell your momma I'll be stopping by for dinner after I close up shop tonight."

CHAPTER SEVEN

The pig ran out of the kitchen.

The 400 lb. porker's hooves clattered on the tiled floor as it scurried into the dining room. A frayed rope was tied around its neck.

La Chichen-Itza's head cook, Fredo Ortega, and his two assistants, chased after it. Rawly's mother ran behind them, her eyes blazing. "Get that pig out of here!"

The pig headed toward a table where a husband and wife and their four-year-old daughter were sitting.

"Eeee!" the little girl screamed. She hopped onto her mother's lap. Her father bolted out of his seat. He grabbed his fork and jabbed the air, trying to fend off the pig. The pig paused to sniff the fork. It took off again when it saw Fredo and his assistants coming after it.

"Get him!" Mrs. Sánchez shrieked. She stopped to apologize to the family before going after the pig again.

The pig ran to another table where two female tellers from the nearby Laredo National Bank were eating an early dinner. The women screamed. They ran inside the mop closet and slammed the door shut.

The pig climbed up their table and helped itself to what was left of their Wednesday enchilada dinner specials.

The rest of the customers scattered, some laughing nervously, others stunned.

Fredo lunged for the rope around the pig's neck but missed. He fell on the floor, belly first. The pig moved out of the way, knocking over the table, and sent it and the dishes crashing on the floor.

At that moment, Rawly and Nevin entered the restaurant. As soon as they opened the door, the pig dashed out.

"What the . . . " Rawly started before he was interrupted by his mother's shouts. Fredo and the assistant cooks ran out the door and chased the pig down the sidewalk.

"Dude, I need to eat here more often," Nevin said dryly.

When the chaos was over, the man, whose daughter had been terrified by the pig, unleashed his anger at Rawly's mother. "What kind of place are you people running here? Is this a restaurant or a farm?"

"I'm sorry. I am so sorry," Mrs. Sánchez whimpered.

"I want to speak to the owner!" the man demanded. "Now!"

"I-I'm Leonor Sánchez."

"Lady, I don't care who you are," the man said, pointing a finger at her face. "I want to speak to Mr. L. A. Chichen-Itza himself."

"I own the restaurant."

"You do? Well, let me tell you something, lady," the man roared. "I have a good mind to call the health department and have them shut you down!"

"Please, I . . . I . . . " Mrs. Sánchez stammered. "Look, don't worry about your bill. Dinner's on the house. You don't have to pay anything."

"I should say so," the man said. "But that's still no excuse for bringing a pig into the restaurant." His eyes grew wide. "Wait a minute. Don't tell me you're cooking live pigs in the kitchen!" He stared at his wife. "Maybe I oughta call the news and have them investigate what's going on back there."

"No! Please, don't do that," Mrs. Sánchez begged.

She stared at the bewildered customers standing around the dining room. Besides the man and his wife and their daughter, there were the two tellers who were peeking out of the mop closet, three parties of four and an old man who was a regular.

"How about some dessert?" Mrs. Sánchez offered. "Maybe some flan or . . . "

"Lady, I wouldn't spend another second eating in this place!" the irate man said. "C'mon, let's get out of here." He and his wife and little girl walked toward the door. "I'm gonna call the news people about this," he threatened before he stalked out.

The rest of the customers, except for the old man, left too.

The old man smiled and said, "Meal's free, right?"

Mrs. Sánchez slumped in a booth, exhausted. She dropped a hand over her face and closed her eyes.

"Where did that pig come from?" Rawly asked, hardly believing what he had just witnessed.

"That fool. That stupid fool," his mother said, her face contorted in agony. "I'm probably going to get shut down because of him."

"Who?"

"Fredo."

"Why did Fredo bring the pig to the restaurant?"

Rawly's mother shuddered. Thoughts of possible lawsuits, visits by the health department and news cameras being shoved in her face raced through her mind.

"Mom?"

"Fredo didn't bring the pig. Mr. Joe did."

Mr. Joe owned a pig farm in Lancaster, just outside of Dallas. He stopped by each morning to collect the food scraps that were thrown away, to feed his pigs.

"Fredo bought the pig from Mr. Joe," Rawly's mother said. "But he thought Mr. Joe was bringing him a pig that was ready to be cut up and cooked. Instead, Mr. Joe brought a live pig." She burst into tears. "Rawly, they're going shut me down. I just know they are."

"I think I'd better go," Nevin said uncomfortably.

"No, please." Mrs. Sánchez composed herself and slid out of the booth. "Sit down. I'll get you something to eat."

At that moment, Fredo walked back inside the restaurant, holding the pig tightly by the short piece of rope around its neck.

When Nevin saw the pig, he quipped, "I don't eat pork."

"Get that pig out of here!" Mrs. Sánchez bellowed.

"I'm sorry, *señora*," Fredo said. "It's just that the pig chewed through the rope and got away from us."

The old man looked down at the pig. "I get free dessert, too, right?"

"Get rid of that pig. Now!"

"*Sí, señora*." Fredo started out the door.

"No! Not through the front. I don't want anyone else to see it. Take the pig out the back."

Rawly's mother wiped her eyes with a napkin and shook her head in disgust. "If I didn't need Fredo so badly, I'd fire him right now."

With a lost look on her face, she dragged herself to her office behind the counter and shut the door.

Rawly wanted to go to her, to comfort her somehow, but he didn't know what to say. He surveyed the mess in the dining room. "Come on, Nevin. Help me get this place cleaned up."

Rawly righted the table the pig had knocked down. He grabbed a dustpan and a broom and swept up the broken dishes while Nevin wiped the table with a wet towel.

"You know, dude, maybe we could work out a skit about a pig for Open Mic Nite," Nevin said. "What do you think?"

Rawly cleared another table and dumped the dishes into a gray plastic tub. "No, Nevin. I am not going to be in Open Mic Nite."

"Come on, Rawls, I need a partner," Nevin said. "I can't do stand-up, but I think I could write a comedy skit."

"No."

After they finished cleaning, they relaxed in a booth. Teresita approached them and asked, "You guys having the special tonight?"

"Sure," Nevin said. "If it's good enough for the pig, it's good enough for me. I'll have an enchilada dinner and a Coke."

"Me too," Rawly said. "But I want mango juice instead of Coke."

"Mango juice?" Nevin said, surprised.

"I like mango juice," Rawly told him. "It's pretty good stuff. You ought to try it some time."

Nevin thought for a moment, and then said, "Okay, I will. Bartender, bring me a glass of mango juice on the rocks."

"Sure thing. I'll bring it right out," Teresita said.

Nevin's face brightened. "Hey, I just thought of an idea for our Open Mic Nite skit. See what you think."

Rawly started to protest but decided to let Nevin talk.

"The Three Little Pigs go out for dinner," Nevin began. "The waiter comes and takes their drink orders.

'I'd like a Coke,' the first little pig says.

'I'd like mango juice,' says the second little pig.

'I just want water, lots and lots of water,' the third little pig says.

The waiter brings them their drinks and takes their dinner orders.

'I want an enchilada dinner,' says the first little pig.

'I want an order of nachos,' says the second little pig.

'I just want water, lots and lots of water,' the third little pig says.

The meals are brought out. Later, the waiter asks if the pigs would like dessert.

'I want some ice cream,' says the first little pig.

'I want some flan,' says the second little pig.

'I just want water, lots and lots of water,' the third little pig says.

Finally the waiter says to the third little pig, 'Pardon me. I don't mean to be nosy, but why have you only ordered water all evening?'

The pig answers, 'Well, somebody has to go wee, wee, wee, all the way home!'" Nevin cracked up.

Rawly groaned. "Oh, brother. That is so stupid."

"Aw, come on, dude. It's funny. You know it is. I could play the waiter. You could play one of the pigs, and I'll ask a couple of other guys if they want to join us. We could probably find pig masks at Ghouls & More."

"No, Nevin," Rawly said, exasperated. "I am not going to dress up like a pig and make a fool of myself in front of everybody."

"All right, scratch the pig idea. How about this, then? What if we did a variation of Chicken Little? You know, the sky is falling! The sky is falling!"

"Will you stop?" Rawly balled up his napkin and tossed it at Nevin. "I am not going to play a pig or a chicken. Or an airhead. I don't want to be in Open Mic Nite."

Nevin leaned back in the booth, crossed his arms and sniffed haughtily. "I guess Miyoko was right about you."

Rawly sat up. "Miyoko? What did she say about me?"

"Oh, nothing." Nevin took the napkin and wrapped it around his head like a scarf. "It's just that when I told her I was going to talk to you about being in a comedy skit with me, she said she didn't think you'd do it."

Rawly wrinkled his brows. "Why would she say that? She doesn't even know me."

"Beats me. She said she didn't think you could be funny onstage."

"I can be funny," Rawly insisted. "If the material's right."

Nevin took the napkin off his head and placed it on his lap. "So you'll do it?"

"Maybe. Depends on what you come up with." Rawly's face grew pensive. "So Miyoko really said that about me? That she didn't think I could funny?"

Nevin shrugged. "Maybe I heard her wrong. She might have said you were funny-looking."

Teresita brought out their food. "Mango juice on the rocks," she said. She poured their drinks from small blue cans into glasses of ice.

Nevin tasted it. "Hey, this stuff is good."

"I told you," Rawly said. "It's Jumex." He pronounced it *Who Mex.*

"Huh?"

"It's a Mexican drink. Jumex is a combination of the words *jugo* and *mexicano*, which mean Mexican juice," Rawly explained. "They sell it in different flavors. Mango happens to be my favorite."

Nevin picked up the little blue can and read the label. "It looks like it says Jew Mex." He grinned. "Hey, this is us, dude. Jumex. You know, Jew and Mexican. We're Jumex."

Rawly laughed.

"Seriously. That's what we'll call ourselves when we do our comedy routine. We'll be known as Jumex."

Rawly took a sip of his drink. "I didn't say I'd do the show."

"But you will," Nevin said. "You don't want Miyoko to think you're not funny, do you?"

That struck a raw nerve. "I *can* be funny," Rawly said. "You just watch."

CHAPTER EIGHT

On Saturday morning, Rawly walked into Mr. Mondragón's classroom and noticed Miyoko sitting by herself in a corner.

I'll show her I can be funny.

He walked up to her desk and said, *"Buenos días, señorita."* He bowed and pretended to remove a hat, the way he had seen Nevin do at the mall.

Miyoko crossed her arms and turned up her nose. "I can't believe we have to spend Saturday morning sitting in here, Raymond. It's not fair."

Rawly straightened. "Uh, my name's Rawly."

"I spend forty-five minutes, five days a week, in this stupid class," Miyoko said. "What does Mr. Mondragón think he's going to teach me on Saturdays that he can't teach me Monday through Friday? You tell me."

Rawly was taken aback. He hadn't seen this side of Miyoko.

"I was supposed to go to the fair with Iris and Amanda today, but my mom's mad at me because she had to get up extra early on a Saturday to drive me to school, and now she says I can't . . . "

Mr. Mondragón entered the classroom. Miyoko uttered something Rawly didn't quite catch. He hoped he was mistaken, but it sounded as if she had used a cuss word to describe their teacher.

After Mr. Mondragón greeted his students, he handed out packets of worksheets. Each sheet contained problems similar to the ones he had assigned during the week.

While Mr. Mondragón wrote a list of algebra terms on the board, Rawly caught Miyoko sticking her tongue out at their teacher.

Rawly checked the time. It was ten after nine. He guessed his mother would be driving past Corsicana by now on her way to Midway.

He thought about Jaime sitting in his cell all week, with nothing to do, looking forward to Saturdays, when he would get to visit with his family. Rawly wished he could have gone to see him. He missed having his brother at home. But things changed forever after Jaime's accident.

Jaime's accident.

That's what his mother always called it. It might have been an accident, but Jaime had still killed that nurse.

On the night of his graduation, Jaime drove to Aaron's apartment. Aaron's parents had gone out for the evening, wanting to give their son a chance to celebrate with his friends. They placed their older son, Victor, in charge of the party.

Jorge was there, along with Gustavo and Rudy. So, too, were five girls and three cases of beer.

They drank and ate. They danced and watched movies.

At around twelve-thirty, Jaime staggered out of the apartment and got in his car. He was drunk, he realized, and he probably shouldn't be on the road. He'd be okay, though. He didn't live that far. He'd be home in less than fifteen minutes.

A light rain had started to fall. Jaime turned on the windshield wipers, but all they did was mix the dirt on his grimy windshield with the rain, leaving arched streaks of mud on the glass.

As he made his way home, a green light up ahead turned yellow. Jaime gunned the gas. He didn't want to get stuck at a red light.

Helen Decamp, a nurse at Methodist Medical Center, had just finished her shift and was on her way home. Approaching the intersection, she slowed down for the red light. The light changed to green before she made a complete stop, so she accelerated her car.

She never saw the Chevy Impala racing toward her.

Jaime slammed on the brakes. His tires screamed. His car skidded on the slick street, and he crashed, almost full force. The nurse's car flipped over twice before coming to a stop on its side.

Jaime had always buckled up before starting his car, but he didn't think to do so when he left the party. His head busted through the windshield, and he flew out of the car, landing twelve feet away, unconscious.

The next thing he remembered was waking up in a hospital bed. His head was bandaged up. His jaw was broken and his mouth was wired shut. An oxygen mask covered his nose and mouth. His mother and brother stood over him, looking downcast.

Jaime later learned that the woman whose car he hit had died at the scene of the accident.

After he was released from the hospital, the police charged Jaime with intoxication manslaughter.

At the trial, a tearful Mike Decamp told the jurors, "Our lives will never be the same. My little girl will have to grow up without her mother, all because of him." He pointed at Jaime.

The trial ended with Jaime being found guilty. The judge in the case had been cracking down on drunk drivers. He sentenced Jaime to fifteen to twenty years in the state penitentiary. He also assessed him a ten thousand dollar fine.

After Jaime went to prison, Mrs. Sánchez gave up her restaurant's liquor license. She could not, in good conscience, sell alcohol after what it had done to her son.

Tutoring class ended.

Rawly tried to catch up with Miyoko, but he lost sight of her in a crowd of students. He spotted her a few minutes later, getting into a car with a woman he presumed was her mother. He couldn't hear what they were saying, but apparently, they were having an argument. Miyoko flailed her arms and yelled. Her mother gripped the steering wheel and stared straight ahead.

Finally, the car tore away from the curb, its tires squealing, and turned the corner sharply at the stop sign.

Rawly crossed the street and made his way to Nevin's house.

CHAPTER NINE

Nevin's mother answered the door. Before greeting Rawly, she looked up at the sky and made a face. "Looks like it's going to rain again," she said, more to herself than to Rawly.

"Hello, Mrs. Steinberg. Is Nevin home?" Rawly asked.

Her eyes remained fixed on the sky a moment longer before she acknowledged him. "Yes. Hi, Rawly. Come in."

She led him past the living room and into the den. The mantle above the fireplace was lined with family pictures, separated by a brass menorah.

Nevin's mother gazed out the glass panels of the French double doors that opened into the patio. "Typical Texas weather," she said, shaking her head. "Can you believe it? We hardly had a drop of rain all summer when we needed it the most. Now, here we are, in the middle of October, and it's rained almost every day for the past two weeks."

"Is that Rawly, Mother?" Nevin called from upstairs.

"Yeah, it's me," Rawly answered.

"Come on up."

Rawly climbed the stairs and walked down the hallway to Nevin's bedroom. The room was empty. Rawly figured Nevin was probably in the bathroom.

Three bookcases across from Nevin's bed were filled with novels, reference materials, and picture books Nevin read when he was little. Mixed in with the books were Nevin's monster toys.

Rawly picked up a model of the endoskeleton from the *Terminator* series. While he studied its features, he thought he heard a scratching sound.

He turned.

The sound seemed to be coming from Nevin's closet.

Rawly placed the toy back on the shelf and listened.

There it was again. A slow, clawing noise. Maybe it was a hanger brushing against the door. But what could be moving the hanger? A draft of air? Inside the closet?

Rawly reached for the doorknob. The scraping sound grew louder, heavier. He recoiled. Goose bumps blossomed on his arms. He looked out the doorway. "Hey, Nevin, I'm in your room."

No answer.

Scra-a-a-tch! Scra-a-a-tch! Scra-a-a-tch!

The small hairs on the back of Rawly's neck prickled.

This is silly. There's no reason to be scared. The only monsters in the room are the toys sitting on Nevin's bookcases.

Rawly reached for the doorknob again.

Scra-a-a-tch! Scra-a-a-tch! Scra-a-a-tch!

His heart palpitated.

He turned the knob.

Slowly, slowly.

The door burst open.

"Aarrgh!" A gorilla jumped out of the closet and seized Rawly by the throat.

"Eeeyagh!" Rawly stumbled backwards and fell, still in the grips of the gorilla.

The gorilla pulled off its mask and laughed hysterically. "Dude, you look *sooo* funny!" Nevin cried.

Embarrassed, Rawly pushed him off and sat up. "What's your problem, man?"

Nevin caught his breath. "I don't have a problem. You do. You don't have a sense of humor." He stood and stretched out his hand to help Rawly up.

Rawly slapped it away and got up on his own. "Where'd you get that costume?"

Nevin unzipped the gorilla outfit and slipped out of it. Underneath, he wore black pants, a white shirt, and a red tie. "It belongs to my dad. You know, he's the PR director at the Dallas Zoo. He's also Safari Bob, game hunter, when he makes school visits." Nevin peered at his reflection on his dresser mirror and brushed back his hair. "He gets volunteers from the zoo to wear the costume to play his assistant, Mortimer the Gorilla."

Rawly seemed to recall Nevin mentioning something about that, but he had never seen the gorilla costume. "What's with the dress shirt and tie?" he asked.

Nevin tucked in his shirt. "My mom's idea. She thinks wearing a tie to the store will help me pick out the right suit."

"Are you going with a black one?"

"Yeah. I thought about what you said. I really do need a black suit, 'cause some old relative of mine's always dying."

"So what are you planning to do with the gorilla costume? Are you going to wear it to a Halloween party or something?"

"No, dude, it's for you."

"For me?"

"Yeah. I thought about a great skit for Open Mic Nite. See what you think." Nevin pulled out the chair from his

desk and sat down. Rawly sat on the bed across from
him. "I'll wear my dad's Safari Bob khaki clothes and pith
helmet, and you'll wear the gorilla outfit," Nevin said.
"I'll play a world-famous game hunter who's caught a
ferocious gorilla."

Rawly smiled. "Sounds like fun. Weird but fun." Despite
what he had said earlier, he was beginning to like the idea
of being onstage with Nevin. And dressed up like a gorilla?
It'd be a riot. He'd show Miyoko he could be funny.

"I won't have to memorize any lines, will I?" Rawly
asked.

"No, dude. You're a gorilla. Gorillas can't talk."

Rawly slipped on the gorilla mask and stared at himself in the mirror. "This is awesome."

"Remember in the movie, *Young Frankenstein*, where
Dr. Frankenstein and the monster sang and danced to
Puttin' on the Ritz?" Nevin asked. "I thought we'd do something similar. We won't sing, but we can work up a dance
routine."

Rawly pulled off the mask. "Wait a minute. I don't
know how to dance."

"Neither do I," Nevin said. "That's what'll make our
skit even funnier."

"Okay, count me in. I'm with you," Rawly said.

"Of course you are," Nevin said. "'Cause we're a team.
We're Jumex."

They made their way downstairs.

"What was all that noise up there?" Nevin's mother
asked. "You boys weren't fighting, were you?"

"No, Mother," Nevin said. "Rawly was showing me
some ballet movements. He says he wants to be a balle-
rina when he grows up."

"That's nice," Mrs. Steinberg said. "Nevin, be sure to wear your windbreaker. And take an umbrella. I don't like the looks of those clouds."

"We'll be fine, Mother."

"Are you sure you don't want me to drive you, honey? I would hate for you to get wet."

"Don't worry about us. We'll be okay."

"When you pick out your suit, button the coat to make sure it fits properly. You don't want it too tight."

"I will, Mother."

"And if the pants are too long, ask them to alter the hem. I don't want you dragging the pant legs."

"Yes, Mother."

"If it should start to rain, you call me, and I'll go get you."

Nevin sighed. "Yes, Mother."

"And if anyone approaches you and asks if you want to buy drugs, you run away and find a security guard, you hear?" She kissed Nevin's cheek.

Nevin slammed the door shut behind them. "¡Ay Chihuahua! I can't handle all that love."

They caught the DART bus a block away. While they rode, Nevin asked, "How was tutoring? Did the Dragon Man teach you anything?"

Rawly groaned. "Nevin, there were times when I thought Mr. Mondragón was speaking a foreign language. Honestly, I don't know how I'm ever going to pass algebra this year."

"Did you think like Batman?" Nevin asked.

"That doesn't work."

"It does for Batman."

"Yeah? Well, tell me this," Rawly said. "How many times have you seen Batman do algebraic word problems?"

Nevin grinned. "You've got me there, dude."

When they arrived at the mall, they stopped by Ghouls & More, a temporary Halloween store, to look at the costumes and decorations. The year before, Rawly and Nevin had attended a Halloween party that was held in their middle school gymnasium. Rawly wore a Captain America costume. Nevin dressed up as a "dead" M&M. He wore a yellow M&M costume with a plastic butcher knife sticking out of the top. Fake blood dripped from the knife.

This year, North Oak Cliff High School was holding a Halloween dance party, where students were encouraged to wear costumes. Rawly and Nevin weren't planning to go to the party, since neither one knew how to dance.

Rawly stared at the grotesque rubber masks hanging behind the counter. He thought about buying one but decided against it. He probably wouldn't be able to wear it anywhere, anyway. This year, Halloween fell on a Wednesday, and there was no way he was going to get to go trick-or-treating. Because of the enchilada dinner special, Wednesday was La Chichen-Itza's busiest day of the week. Like it or not, Rawly would be spending Halloween night cleaning tables.

What if he wore one of those masks while he worked? Maybe the evil clown one with the vampire teeth and the large bloody gash splitting his forehead down the middle. Or the zombie mask with the rotting flesh and an eyeball hanging from its socket. Nah. Rawly wouldn't have the mask on more than two minutes before his mother would make him take it off.

Nevin walked up to him, holding a life-size rubber skeleton. "Dude, check this out." He covered the skeleton's eyes with its hands, and then quickly pulled them away. "Peek-a-boo!" He did it again. "Peek-a-boo!"

"Yeah, that's real funny," Rawly said, rolling his eyes. "Listen, Nevin, you go on to Penney's without me. I'll wait for you here."

Nevin tossed the skeleton on a table. "No, dude. I need your help picking out my suit. That's why I brought you with me."

"I can't go back inside Penney's," Rawly said. "That clerk might be watching out for me. Thanks to you, she thinks I'm a weirdo. Besides, you already know what you're going to buy."

"Come on, Rawls," Nevin said. "That old scarecrow works in the ladies' department. She's probably not even here today. And even if she is, she won't see you." He smiled impishly and added, "As long as you stay away from the ladies' underwear."

"Look, Nevin, if you're going to start with that," Rawly fumed, "I'll get on the bus right now and go back home."

"Aw, chill out, dude," Nevin said. "I'm just yanking your chain. Come on. Let's go buy a suit."

When they entered Penney's, Rawly looked around for the old saleswoman, but he didn't see her.

Nevin rummaged through a rack of suits until he found one his size. He grabbed a black Stafford suit and went inside the dressing room to try it on.

When he came out, he stood in front of a three-panel mirror and admired himself. "What do you think?"

"Not bad," Rawly said. "You look like you're ready for the Easter Parade."

Nevin frowned. "We don't celebrate Easter, Rawls. You know that."

"Chill out, dude," Rawly said. "I'm just yanking your chain."

Rawly didn't mean to make fun of Nevin's religion. That comment came out of nowhere. It was something his *güelo* González used to say to him whenever Rawly got all dressed up.

Nevin buttoned his coat and strolled around the men's section, trying to get a feel for his new clothes.

While he stared at himself in a mirror hanging on one of the columns, a chubby, middle-aged woman walked up to him and said, "Excuse me, young man. Do you work here?"

Nevin covered the price tag on the coat's sleeve. "Why, yes, I do. I am one of the assistant managers. How may I help you?"

The woman asked, "Can you tell me where the ladies' plus sizes are?"

"Yes, of course," Nevin said. "The elephants' section is upstairs."

Rawly's mouth fell open.

The woman's face flushed red. "What did you say?"

Nevin smiled innocently. "I said the elegant section is upstairs. I assume you are looking for something elegant to wear. We have many lovely selections for you to choose from."

With a baffled look on her face, the woman said, "Yes. Thank . . . thank you." She walked away, unsure of what she had heard.

Rawly laughed nervously. "That was cold, man."

"You take life too seriously, dude," Nevin said with a shameless grin. "I just try to bring a little humor into this dreary world. Come on. Let's go pay for this get-up."

CHAPTER TEN

Rawly shifted uneasily in his chair. His eyes were fixed on the failing notice in his hand. He had been expecting it, but still, it surprised him when his teacher handed it to him.

"This is your copy," Mr. Mondragón said. "Your parents will receive an official one in the mail." He pushed aside a half-eaten sandwich from his desk and opened a bag of potato chips.

"But I've started coming to tutoring, sir," Rawly said. "I'm trying to get better at algebra."

Mr. Mondragón smiled, exposing a gap between his upper front teeth. "I know you are, son, and I have no doubt that your grades will improve. But district policy says I have to notify the parents if a student is not passing after the third six weeks. Would you like a chip?"

Rawly waved off the bag.

Mr. Mondragón shoved a handful of potato chips into his mouth. "The notice doesn't necessarily mean you're going to fail," he said. "It's just to let you and your parents know where you stand at this point." Flakes of chips escaped from Mr. Mondragón's mouth as he spoke, and Rawly watched them land on a stack of papers. "Have one of your parents sign the notice and return it to me by Friday."

Parent, Rawly thought. Not parents. But he didn't correct his teacher. Mr. Mondragón had over a hundred twenty-five students. Rawly doubted he knew all of them by name, much less anything about their personal lives.

He could explain to his teacher that he didn't have a father, and that one of the reasons he was doing poorly in algebra was because he had to work every night at his mother's restaurant. But what could Mr. Mondragón do about it? Help him clean tables?

Rawly peeked out the door, thinking Nevin might be waiting for him in the hallway. "Is there anything else I can do to bring up my grade?" he asked hopefully.

Mr. Mondragón chomped on more potato chips. "Sure. Turn off the TV. And don't spend all your time playing video games or talking on the phone. Use that time to go over your work. Maybe you'll start seeing a change in your grades." He held out the potato chips bag again. "Sure you don't want some? They're barbeque."

"No, thanks." Rawly stood and headed for the door.

"Don't forget." Mr. Mondragón pretended to press a remote control button. "Click! Click! No TV tonight."

Rawly couldn't recall the last time he had sat down to watch a TV show. Sometimes he and his mother watched the late-night news after they got home from the restaurant. On occasion, he watched a little television on the weekends. But except for the Dallas Cowboys football games, there was little else on TV that interested him. And video games? He wouldn't even know how to begin playing one.

Rawly had managed to keep his head above water in his other subjects—English, social studies, even science

—probably because they mostly involved reading. And Rawly could read, though admittedly, he preferred to read comic books. Algebra, on the other hand, was like learning a new language—a language made up of strange words and numbers.

He read his failing notice again. YOUR CHILD IS IN DANGER OF FAILING DUE TO POOR PERFORMANCE IN CLASS WORK AND ON TESTS.

Rawly had tried studying at the restaurant, but it was almost impossible to concentrate there. In addition to his regular duties, he greeted customers at the door and seated them if his mother was busy.

After Rawly left Mr. Mondragón's classroom, he found Nevin outside on the school steps talking with Miyoko and Iris.

"Dude, I was just telling the girls about our skit for Open Mic Nite."

Miyoko said, "I think it'll be hilarious. Yours will be the best act in the show."

Rawly smiled proudly. "See? And you said I couldn't be funny."

Miyoko looked at him curiously. "I never said you couldn't be funny. Who told you that?"

Nevin cleared his throat. "Well, you know how some people are. They're always making up crazy stuff like that."

"I'm going to play *Moon River* on my clarinet for Open Mic Nite," Iris told the group, but no one paid attention her.

"Where were you anyway, dude?" Nevin asked. "I was worried you might've gotten flushed down the toilet. I was getting ready to go inside the bathroom to rescue you."

The girls laughed.

Rawly felt his face turn red. "I wasn't in the bathroom. Mr. Mondragón wanted to talk to me after class for a few minutes."

"I think I know what it was about, Ronnie," Miyoko said. "I had one of those talks with Mr. Mondragón during third period."

"It's Rawly. My name's Rawly."

Miyoko opened her purse and pulled out a failing notice. "Does this look familiar?"

Nevin shook his head. "Ay, ay, ay. You see? This is what you get for not listening to me. It is so simple. You've got to think like Batman."

Rawly started to answer with something sarcastic, but a better idea came to him. He told Miyoko, "Um, since we're in the same boat and everything, I was wondering if maybe we could, you know, study our algebra together or something." He shrugged. "I mean, we *are* in the same Saturday morning tutoring class, right? What do you think?"

Before Miyoko could respond, Iris said, "I can help you if you'd like, Rawly. I'm not an algebra whiz or anything, but my grades are usually in the high eighties, low nineties."

Nevin caught the awkward look in Rawly's eyes. "I think that's a great idea, Iris," he said. "You can help Rawly and I'll help Miyoko."

Rawly gave him a why-don't-you-keep-your-mouth-shut glare.

"Sure," Iris said. "Rawly, I can get together with you any time before school or maybe during lunch. You can even come to my house after school, if you'd like. Of course, I'll have to check with my mom first."

"Dude, you are so lucky," Nevin said with fake sincerity. "With Iris helping you, not only will you pass algebra, you'll probably end up on the honor roll." He wrapped an arm around Miyoko. "And as for you, young lady, you will have the benefit of being tutored by the great Professor Steinberg himself, mathematician extraordinaire."

Rawly's stomach knotted up. Nevin knew how he felt about Miyoko. Or at least, he should. Nevin was mocking him, purposely keeping Miyoko away from him. Maybe he wanted her for himself after all.

"I can meet you in the cafeteria tomorrow morning at seven-thirty, if that's okay," Iris told Rawly. "That way, we'll have at least an hour to work."

Yeah, sure," Rawly muttered.

"Yippy doodle!" Nevin cried. "I am so happy for you, dude. Iris will make an excellent tutor. Now you won't have to worry about failing algebra."

"And you're going to help me pass, too, right?" Miyoko said.

"But of course, my cherry blossom. Your wish is my command."

Miyoko pushed Nevin away when she saw her mother's car pulling up to the curb.

After the girls left, Rawly glowered at Nevin. "Thanks a lot, man. Thanks a whole hairy lot."

"What's the matter, dude?" Nevin asked, trying to hold back a smile. "I thought I was helping you. I mean, you're the one who's bombing out in algebra."

"You know exactly what I'm talking about," Rawly said.

"Oh. You mean that little scene with Miyoko?" Nevin patted Rawly on the back. "Dude, I'm just trying to save you from yourself."

"What?"

"That's right. Look, Rawls, I hate to burst your little bubble, but you're way out of your league if you think you have a chance with Miyoko Elena."

Rawly's face filled with indignation. "You don't know that."

"Of course I do . . . *Ronnie!*"

Rawly sneered at him and said sharply, "You always have the answers to everything, don't you? Well, then tell me this, Nevin Steinberg. How does it feel to be the smartest person in the whole world? To know more than anyone else?" He kicked a Coke can someone had thrown on the ground and sent it flying into the street. "Maybe I'm not the genius you are, but at least I know how to treat my friends."

Nevin stepped back and calmly replied, "Do you know why the algebra book went to see a therapist? Because it had problems. Get over yourself, dude. I'll see you when you get control of your emotions."

With that, he walked away.

CHAPTER ELEVEN

A Channel 12 News truck was parked in front of La Chichen-Itza Mexican Restaurant. A reporter Rawly recognized from TV as Delia Franco stood under the green awning of Rosario's Salón de Belleza next door, while a cameraman videotaped her.

"This year, the State Fair of Texas is once again featuring the popular pig races," Delia Franco said into her microphone. "Those speedy little hogs race around a track while the crowds cheer them on. However, according to eyewitnesses, another kind of pig race was held here at La Chichen-Itza Mexican Restaurant in Oak Cliff."

Rawly was shocked. The man had actually carried out his threat to call the news. Rawly ducked away from the cameraman and the reporter and snuck inside the restaurant.

His mother stood at the window, peeking through the blinds. Teresita, Isabel, and Fredo stood with her.

The restaurant was empty, which was normal for that time of day. Except for Wednesdays, when the enchilada dinner special was offered, customers didn't usually show up in the evenings until after five.

"How long have they been out there?" Rawly asked his mother.

She didn't answer. Anguish and fear filled her face.

"They arrived a little while ago," Isabel whispered. "Unannounced. They tried to interview your mom, but she kicked them out."

Rawly's mother whirled around and scowled. "Shh!"

Isabel gave her an apologetic expression.

For the next few minutes, everyone watched in silence.

Finally, Mrs. Sánchez pulled herself away from the window. She let out a long sigh. Her shoulders slumped, as if all the air in her body had escaped. Her face was drained of color. "They're gone, *gracias a Dios.*"

She looked old to Rawly, much older than her forty-three years. Folds of skin sagged below her eyes. Her makeup, which she usually applied with great care, now looked caked on, like a circus clown's.

Mrs. Sánchez's life was the restaurant. It had been that way ever since she opened it ten years ago. Rawly couldn't understand why she worked so hard to hang on to the restaurant. It had never made any money.

He hated working there—bussing tables every evening, plus having to do a million other chores. No wonder he stunk at algebra.

His mother couldn't pay him a regular salary, either. Something about child labor laws preventing her from putting him on the payroll. She did give him a few dollars a week for spending money. Not that it did him any good. Except for a couple of hours here and there when he had a chance to go to the mall or to Heroes & Villains, he hardly had any free time to spend it.

Rawly doubted Jaime would want to help run the restaurant once he got out of prison, and that wouldn't happen for fifteen to twenty years. The lawyers had been somewhat hopeful. They told Rawly's mother that there was a possibility Jaime could be released in about seven years. Rawly wondered if La Chichen-Itza would even be around in seven years.

The pig getting loose in the restaurant might have a blessing in disguise. Maybe it would be best if the restaurant did shut down. Then his mother could get a job that didn't require her to work eighty to ninety hours a week.

Rawly looked across the dining room. His mother sat in a booth, tapping away at her laptop. The restaurant, he thought, was slowly sapping the life out of her.

It had long been his parents' dream to own a restaurant. They used to talk about it all the time, back when they both waited tables at La Paloma Blanca in Marsville, Texas. Their boss, Mingo Salazar, had been encouraging and supportive, offering them valuable advice on how to succeed in the restaurant business.

Rawly's father came up with the restaurant's name as a tribute to his home state of Quintana Roo on the Yucatán Peninsula in Mexico, near the archaeological site of Chichen-Itza.

In the end, though, it was nothing more than a dream. Rawly's parents had no money to open up a restaurant, not even a *taquería*. Their combined tips barely paid the bills, and the banks were not eager to lend them money based on their meager salaries.

Then Rawly's father died.

It started with a cough—a mild, irritating, hacking cough his father thought would go away in a day or two. When it didn't, he drank some cough syrup, thinking the medicine would take care of the problem. Still, his coughing continued. His wife urged him to see a doctor, but he refused. It was just a cough, for goodness' sakes. Besides, they didn't have money to spend on doctors.

In the days that followed, Rawly's father's cough worsened. Mingo Salazar threatened to send him home if he didn't see a doctor, because his coughing was grossing out the customers.

Rawly's father visited a clinic he had seen advertised on TV. A young doctor prescribed an antibiotic and a prescription cough syrup and sent him home.

But the coughing didn't go away.

Growing desperate, Rawly's father checked himself in at Landry Memorial Hospital. Finally, after a thorough examination and a series of tests, the doctor delivered the most shocking and unexpected news.

"I'm afraid you have lung cancer."

Lung cancer? Rawly's father gaped at the doctor in disbelief. How could he have lung cancer? He didn't even smoke.

The doctor went on to explain that Rawly's father may have contracted lung cancer from second-hand smoke working at La Paloma Blanca. Then, as if the lung cancer announcement wasn't devastating enough, the doctor added, "You have, at most, six months to live."

Six months!

That was all the time Rawly's father had left in the world.

When he shared the news with his wife, her immediate reaction was to file a lawsuit against Mingo Salazar and La Paloma Blanca, but Rawly's father talked her out of it. Mingo had been a good boss. It wasn't Mingo's fault he had lung cancer.

Rawly's father pulled out a life insurance policy he had bought from the Lone Star Life Insurance Company and studied it. An insurance agent named Ramos or Ramirez had shown up at their door one day and talked him into buying the policy. Rawly's father had been reluctant to purchase it at first. Why did he need life insurance? He had planned to live for a long time. The insurance man convinced him to buy the policy, reminding him that life offers no guarantees.

The value of the policy would cover the cost of his funeral; it would also leave his wife with enough money to start her own restaurant.

After Rawly's father died, Mrs. Sánchez quit her job at La Paloma Blanca and moved her family to Dallas. She leased a building that had once been a restaurant called Maggie's Kitchen and converted it into La Chichen-Itza.

Rawly's mother decided her restaurant would be smoke-free, even if it meant losing customers. As it turned out, Dallas already had a law that did not allow smoking in any of its restaurants.

The non-smoking policy hadn't hurt her business. It was only after Rawly's mother gave up her liquor license that customers started to disappear. People wanted to enjoy their Mexican food with a cold beer or a margarita. Now it appeared that the restaurant would finally be done in by, of all things, a pig.

Rawly thought back to something Jaime had said during their last visit.

Look at these guys, 'manito. They're a bunch of losers. Do you want to end up like them? Like me? A loser?

We're all losers, Jaime, Rawly thought sadly. Dad died of lung cancer even though he didn't smoke. You killed a woman without meaning to. I'm flunking algebra, and Mom's about to lose the restaurant over a stupid pig.

Rawly felt the need to pray, but nothing came out. He and his mother seldom attended church. Sundays were spent at the restaurant. They did try to make it to the big church events—Christmas, Easter, and of course, Mother's Day, but that was about it.

Rawly figured they would have to go to church a lot more often than that before God would bother to listen to his prayers. On the other hand, what did he have to lose? Rawly tried praying again. This time the words that came to him were: Hail Mary, full of Grace. Bless us losers in this place.

CHAPTER TWELVE

Nevin's mother pulled up to the curb in front of the school. Heavy rains and high winds swirled around her car. The severe storms had begun to flood the streets.

"I'm sorry, dear, but this is as close as I can get," she told Nevin.

"That's okay. I can make it from here."

"Are you sure?"

"Yes, Mother, I'm sure."

"Try not to get the costumes wet, especially the gorilla outfit. You know, I practically had to beg your father to let you borrow it."

"Yes, Mother. You've told me that about a hundred times already."

"No need to get snippy with me, Nevin. Just be careful with it. That costume cost a lot of money, you know."

"Yes, Mother."

"Do you have on your galoshes?"

Nevin showed her his feet.

"And your umbrella?"

"Right here."

"Try to avoid the mud puddles, if you can."

"I will, Mother."

Nevin jumped out of the car. Gripping the umbrella in one hand and the garment bag in the other, he sloshed his way to the school's main entrance. His clothes were drenched. Nevin would have to switch into his Safari Bob costume right away.

Rawly waited for him outside the auditorium. He had been debating whether he would go through with Open Mic Nite. Originally he had agreed to take part in the program to prove to Miyoko that he could be funny. He realized now that she couldn't care less if he was funny. She couldn't care less if he existed. Rawly had tried to talk to her again on Saturday after tutoring class, but she abruptly cut him off and left to hang out with her friends.

"You're way out of your league if you think you have a chance with Miyoko Elena."

Nevin was right. Girls like Miyoko didn't go for boring, going-nowhere, loser, comic-book geeks. They went for football jocks like Cruz Vega or witty, charming guys like Nevin Steinberg.

Rawly peeked inside the auditorium. Miyoko was sitting in the front row, tuning her guitar. Iris was with her, along with a few other Open Mic Nite participants. Rawly wanted to talk to Miyoko, but why bother? He was invisible to her. She couldn't even remember his name.

Maybe he would go down there and start up a conversation with Iris. She had been helping him with his algebra. He could talk to her about that. If Miyoko said anything, he could ease into a conversation with her.

He walked down the aisle.

Iris was playing her scales on her clarinet. She looked up and smiled. "Hi, Rawly. Are you ready for tonight?"

"Sure. As soon as Nevin gets here with my costume."

"I can hardly wait for your act," Miyoko said. "You're going to look so funny dancing onstage, dressed like a gorilla."

Rawly beamed. "Yeah?"

"I think you guys are pretty gutsy to get up there to do something like that, Rawly," she said.

"My name's . . . " Rawly started before realizing that Miyoko had called him by his name. "Yeah, uh, thanks. How about you? What are you playing tonight?"

"*Moon River*," Iris answered. "Listen." She played a few bars on her clarinet.

"I was asking Miyoko," Rawly said.

"*Bésame Mucho*."

Rawly's face grew hot. Had Miyoko just told him to kiss her?

"It's an old song my dad taught me," Miyoko clarified.

A song. She wasn't telling him to kiss her.

"It goes like this." Miyoko strummed her guitar and sang, "*Bésame, bésame mucho. Como si fuera ésta noche la última vez. Bésame, bésame mucho. Que tengo miedo perderte, perderte después.*"

Rawly swooned at the sound of her voice. And those words! *Kiss me; kiss me many times, as if this was our last night together. Kiss me; kiss me many times, for I have a fear of losing you later on.*

When she finished, Rawly applauded. "You sound like a professional."

Miyoko shrugged modestly. "Thank you, Rawly."

There! She said his name again.

"Did you get a chance to go over the algebraic formulas I showed you this morning?" Iris asked Rawly.

Algebraic formulas? We don't need no steenkin' algebraic formulas.

"No, not yet," Rawly said. "But I will."

"How are things working out with Iris tutoring you, Rawly?" Miyoko asked.

He smiled. "All right, I guess."

"Rawly's a good student," Iris told her. "I think he's going to survive algebra after all. How about you, cuz? Has Nevin been able to help you?"

Miyoko placed her guitar back in its case. "Not really. We got together a couple of times, but Nevin mostly sat around cracking jokes. For example, when a problem said to find x, Nevin drew an arrow pointing to the x and wrote, here it is."

"That's Nevin for you," Rawly said. "He doesn't take anything seriously." A tinge of guilt came over him. He wondered if he was betraying Nevin by talking bad about him. Still, how did the old saying go? All's fair in love and war.

He had an idea. "Why don't you join us for tutoring, Miyoko?" he asked. "Iris has been a great help to me. She can teach you a lot more about algebra than Nevin ever will."

Iris flinched. An uneasy look appeared in her eyes. "Sure. We're, um, meeting tomorrow morning in the cafeteria around seven-thirty, cuz," she said flatly. "You're welcome to join us if you want."

"Maybe," Miyoko said. "I'll ask my mom if she can drop me off at school that early."

"By the way, is Tía Kimi coming tonight?" Iris asked.

"Yes, and she's bringing Granny Sayuki," Miyoko said. "Granny Sayuki wanted me to sing a Japanese song, but I can barely speak the language. I'm a lot more comfortable with Spanish."

Rawly said, "I think the song you're going to sing tonight will . . . "

"*George, George, George of the jungle, strong as he can be,*" Nevin sang as he strolled down the aisle. "*Watch out for that treeee!*" He gazed around the auditorium through his binoculars. "Anyone see any gorillas in here?" He stopped in front of Rawly and aimed his binoculars at him. "Ah, here you are." He turned the binoculars to Miyoko, then back to Rawly. "I see you're still up to the same old monkey business," he said with a wink.

Rawly ignored his comment. "Did you bring my costume?"

Nevin held up the garment bag. "No, dude, I brought you a sack of bananas. Of course I brought your costume. We can't do the show without it."

"Can I see it?" Miyoko asked.

"Why, *soitenly,*" Nevin answered in a high voice, imitating Curly from the Three Stooges. He unzipped the garment bag and pulled out the mask. "Here you go, Rawls. Put it on. It'll improve your looks."

Rawly slipped on the mask. Then he pounded his chest and roared.

The girls laughed.

Nevin asked, "Do you know why gorillas have large nostrils? Because they have large fingers."

"Put on the rest of the costume, Rawly," Miyoko said excitedly.

Nevin noticed people filing into the auditorium. "Uh, you'd better not," he said. "I want to keep it as a surprise."

At seven o'clock, Mr. Hair, the principal, welcomed the audience. He turned the program over to Ms. Coleman, the drama teacher, who was coordinating Open Mic Nite. She introduced the first participants.

Andrea Marino sang *Stormy Weather*, while Nicole Chadima accompanied her on the piano. After that, Santiago Pérez recited Edgar Allan Poe's *Annabel Lee*. Iris Solís followed with her clarinet solo of *Moon River*. The audience applauded politely for each performer.

Things became frenzied when Michelle McCutcheon and her all-girl band took the stage to sing AC/DC's *Highway to Hell*. The girls wore black T-shirts that stopped above their stomachs, short denim skirts and black fishnet hose. Michelle played rhythm guitar, Lisa Kirksey, the bass, Falesha Coe, the keyboard, and Criselda Cobos, the drums.

Mr. Hair had no hair, but if he did, it would have stood on end as he listened to Michelle and her band belt out, *"I'm on the highway to hell, on the highway to hell, m-m-m-m, don't stop me!"*

The auditorium grew calmer but still lively when Travis McHenry and Daniel Vásquez performed "Dead Parrot Sketch," a popular comedy skit from the old British TV show, *Monty Python's Flying Circus*.

Rawly watched from the back. The skit was about an angry customer who had been sold a dead Norwegian Blue parrot and what happened when he tried to return the bird to the shopkeeper. Travis and Daniel delivered their lines with almost perfect British accents.

Rawly spotted Miyoko in the front row. Ms. Coleman had asked the Open Mic Nite participants to sit with the audience, where they would wait until it was their turn to perform. Nevin had requested that he and Rawly be allowed to remain in the back, because he didn't want people to see their costumes until it was time for them to go onstage.

When Travis and Daniel finished, Ms. Coleman took the microphone and announced, "Next, we have the team of . . . Jumex—Nevin Steinberg and Rawly Sánchez. Here they are to perform for you, 'A Mangled Tango.'"

Nevin appeared alone in front of the closed curtains.

"Good evening, ladies and gentlemen. I am Safari Steinberg, renowned game hunter. Throughout the years, I have caught and tamed some of the wildest, fiercest, creatures in the world—the barayakas of Borneo, the menaboras of Madagascar and even the vengatores of Vanuatu. Recently, my travels took me to the remote jungles on the island of Bonga Longa in South America, where I managed to capture the most ferocious, the most vicious, the most terrifying beast the world has never known—the black sable ape of Bonga Longa. Ladies and gentlemen, I present to you . . . *El Bruto!*"

The curtains opened. Rawly, dressed in the gorilla costume, was chained, hands and feet, to two tall, white, plaster columns. The plastic chains had been painted silver to look like metal. Rawly let out a loud roar. The audience laughed and applauded. As he pretended to struggle against the chains, Rawly looked down at Miyoko. She laughed harder than anyone.

I do have a chance with her. Rawly could hardly wait to talk with her after the show.

"Do not be alarmed, dear patrons," Nevin said. "El Bruto cannot harm you. Even his incredible strength is not enough to break the titanium chains that bind him." He looked at the gorilla and said, "Bruto! Be calm!"

The gorilla stopped roaring.

Nevin patted it on the head. "Unlike other game hunters, who use a vast arsenal of weapons to capture their prey, these are the only weapons I need." Nevin pointed to his eyes. "You see, I also possess the uncanny ability to hypnotize animals. Allow me to demonstrate."

He stood in front of the gorilla. "Bruto, look into my eyes."

The gorilla stared at Nevin.

"Deeper. Deeper."

The gorilla slowly closed its eyes. Its head dropped, and its body went limp.

"Good." Nevin turned back to the audience. "El Bruto is now under my total control. He must do exactly as I say." Nevin undid the gorilla's chains. He took it by the hand and led it away from the plaster columns. "Watch as El Bruto obeys my every command. Bruto, sit!"

The gorilla grabbed a chair, sat down and crossed its arms and legs.

The audience laughed and clapped.

"Good, Bruto. Now beg!"

The gorilla pulled out a cardboard sign that read: WILL WORK FOR FOOD.

More laughter.

Rawly drank up the attention. Inside the gorilla costume, he felt so free, so uninhibited. After all, he wasn't performing in front of the audience. The gorilla was. He saw Miyoko enjoying every minute of it. Wait till she saw what came next.

"And now, ladies and gentlemen, I will demonstrate the full extent of my hypnotic abilities," Nevin said. "I will command this once fierce, uncontrollable beast to perform in a remarkable way, the likes of which it has never done."

The stage lights went out.

When they came back on, Nevin and the gorilla had one arm wrapped around each other. With fingers locked, they held their other arms outstretched. The gorilla's head was tilted back, and it held a long-stemmed rose in its mouth. The tango song, *Por Una Cabeza*, began to play. Nevin and the gorilla glided across the stage. When they reached the end, they pivoted, cheek-to-cheek, and danced to the other side. Neither Nevin nor Rawly knew anything about dancing the tango, except what they had seen in movies, but it didn't matter. This was strictly for laughs. Nevin had borrowed the music from his mother's CD collection.

Rawly almost fell when Nevin tried to dip him. The soles of the gorilla costume's feet were made out of a slick, vinyl material. He managed to hold on to Nevin's neck to keep from falling.

He didn't have as much success when Nevin twirled him around a few seconds later. The first time they did the twirl, they executed the move perfectly. When Nevin spun him around the second time, Rawly lost his balance. He whipped his arms to try to straighten back up, but his momentum carried him to the edge of the stage.

"Whoa!"

Rawly hopped off and skidded across the concrete floor. His feet went out from under him, and he fell— right on top of Miyoko!

She shrieked.

Rawly pushed himself off her lap. To his horror, he saw that he had crushed Miyoko's guitar, and the strings had sprung loose from the bridge. Miyoko's eyes and mouth widened with shock.

Granny Sayuki hopped out of her seat and ran down the aisle. She gestured wildly with her arms and spewed angry Japanese words at the clumsy gorilla. Mr. Hair and Ms. Coleman ran down to the front.

Rawly didn't know what to do. People were pointing and laughing. Travis McHenry and Daniel Vásquez rolled in their seats and howled.

Rawly looked at Nevin, who had a big stupid grin on his face. He turned back to Miyoko. Mr. Hair, Ms. Coleman and Miyoko's mother surrounded her, checking to see if she was all right. Granny Sayuki grabbed the broken guitar. She waved it at Rawly and yelled more words he didn't understand.

Rawly's head swiveled around to the audience. To Miyoko. To Nevin. Laughter rang throughout the auditorium.

Humiliated and embarrassed, Rawly raced up the stage steps and disappeared behind the curtain. Backstage, Nevin doubled over with laughter. "Dude, what were you trying to do out there? Play musical chairs?"

Rawly tore off the mask and flung it at him. "Shut up, Nevin!"

Nevin stepped back.

Rawly stripped off the rest of the costume and got dressed. He threw open the school doors, and ran outside.

He wished he had never agreed to be on Open Mic Nite. He wasn't a performer. He hated being onstage. Guys like Nevin hungered for attention, thrived on it. But not him.

When he was in the fourth grade, Rawly had been chosen to play Father Miguel Hidalgo, the famed hero of Mexico's independence, in his school's Cinco de Mayo program. He had to ring the bell of a wooden mission façade and shout, "Down with bad government! Down with the gachupines! Long live Our Lady of Guadalupe!" His last line was supposed to be the cue for the choir to start singing *El Grito de Dolores.* Rawly practiced his lines every day for a week.

On the night of the program, he walked onstage wearing a priest's robe. He grabbed the bell rope and stood in front of the microphone. When he saw the packed auditorium, he froze. He rang the bell, but no words came out of his mouth.

Mr. Dibbles, the choir director, motioned for him to start speaking, but Rawly remained mute as a stone. He kept yanking the rope, ringing the bell, with an idiotic look of fear on his face.

Again Mr. Dibbles signaled for him to say his lines, but Rawly stayed clammed up, saucer-eyed, with his right arm moving up and down. Mr. Dibbles shook his head testily. Finally he gestured for Ms. Haas to start playing the piano.

While the choir sang, Rawly, still in his hypnotic state, continued ringing the bell. Mr. Dibbles led the choir with one hand. With the other, he tried to shoo him off the stage.

Rawly gave the rope a final tug. The wooden structure leaned forward. Then it toppled and fell on him.

Ooohs echoed throughout the auditorium.

Rawly made a grab for the wooden façade, but it was too heavy for him. He managed to scoot from under it and let it go. The church mission crashed on the stage with a heavy clap. The bell broke off and rolled onto the floor with a resounding *clang-clang-clang-clang.*

Mr. Dibbles jumped up onstage to check on Rawly. He gave the audience an apologetic smile. Then he righted the structure and escorted Rawly off.

After the show, the enraged director blasted Rawly. He accused him of being irresponsible, of not caring about the program. He told Rawly that he had let everyone down. Rawly had never been so humiliated in his entire life.

Until tonight.

If he ever thought he stood a chance with Miyoko Elena, he blew it for good. He could still see the expression of disbelief in her eyes when he plopped his big fat gorilla butt on top of her. Not only did he destroy her guitar, he kept her from performing that beautiful Spanish song. Worse, he had embarrassed Miyoko in front of her family and everyone else in the auditorium.

Rawly sat on the bus stop bench, ignoring the rain that poured down on him. His insides burned with anger. With shame. With disgrace. He hunched over, buried his face in his hands and cried.

CHAPTER THIRTEEN

The next day, Rawly didn't meet Iris for tutoring. He didn't want to face Miyoko in case she showed up. He thought about what he might say if he saw her, but he didn't think she would be in any mood to listen.

When he entered first period English class, Travis McHenry winked at Daniel Vásquez and asked, "Hey, Daniel, why did the gorilla cross the road?"

"I don't know, Travis," Daniel said, snickering. "Why *did* the gorilla cross the road?"

"To sit on Miyoko's guitar!" Travis burst out laughing.

"What happened to you last night . . . *El Bruto*?" Daniel mocked. "Did you slip on a banana peel or something?"

"Gorillas shouldn't eat bananas while they're dancing," Travis said, wagging a finger in Rawly's face. "Didn't momma Bruto ever teach you that?"

The teasing continued all day.

"Hey, Rawly, what's black, hairy and dangerous? A gorilla that can't dance!"

"Roses are red, violets are blue, gorillas can't dance, and neither can you!"

Nevin caught up with him between classes. "Hiya, dude. Heard any good jokes lately?"

Rawly stared straight ahead and kept walking. "Get lost, Steinberg!"

"Steinberg?" Nevin raised an eyebrow. "Ooh, why so formal? I thought we were on a first-name basis."

Rawly sped up. He rounded the corner and headed toward the stairs.

Miyoko and some other girls were standing at the foot of the steps, talking. One of the girls saw him. She said something to the others. They all turned and glared at him.

Rawly circled back and walked past Nevin. This time Nevin didn't try to follow him.

Later, while Rawly was taking his books out of his locker Iris approached him and said, "It wasn't your fault, you know. It could've happened to anyone."

Rawly slammed the locker door shut. He looked pitifully at her and said, "But I busted Miyoko's guitar."

Iris shrugged. "Accidents happen. Anyway, it was an old, cheap guitar my uncle picked up at a *mercado* in Mexico. He was planning to buy her a better quality one for Christmas."

Rawly adjusted his books in his arms. "I guess Miyoko's pretty mad at me, huh?"

"She'll get over it," Iris said. "By the way, I missed you in tutoring this morning."

Rawly had already planned to stop meeting Iris for tutoring. Some of the guys had seen them together in the cafeteria and had wondered about them. Arlie Hoyle asked Rawly if Iris was his girlfriend. Things might have been different if Miyoko had joined them, but that wasn't likely to happen now.

"Yeah, well, I probably shouldn't be wasting any more of your time," Rawly said. "I mean, I appreciate you trying to help me and everything, but I'm still flunking algebra. I guess I'm just not any good at it."

"Don't say that, Rawly. You're a lot smarter than you realize." Iris winked at him. "Trust me. You just need a little confidence to get you going. Anyway, you're not wasting my time. I like helping you. But if you can't make it to tutoring, I understand."

When school was out, Rawly caught the DART bus and rode to the restaurant. He stared out the window at the wet, gray world. Rain had fallen intermittently throughout the day. It wasn't raining at the moment, but Rawly knew those thick, dark clouds could open up at any time. He hoped the rain would hold off until he made it to the restaurant.

Rawly wondered if anybody had given Nevin a hard time over the Open Mic Nite mess. If they did, he probably laughed it off.

Nevin was right. Rawly did take life too seriously. Rawly wished he could be more like Nevin. Nothing ever bothered him. But then, why should it? Nevin was outgoing, witty and smarter than anyone Rawly knew. He sometimes wondered why Nevin even hung out with him.

Rawly thought back to seventh grade, when he and Nevin first met. That was when Nevin had saved him from Charlie Matuszak.

Charlie Matuszak was a fifteen-year-old Neanderthal, with an oversized forehead and frog eyes, who took delight in making Rawly's life miserable. Rawly had never said or done anything to provoke Charlie, but it didn't matter. Guys like Charlie Matuszak didn't need a reason to pick on other kids. Charlie was a two-time flunky, who decided that as long as he wasn't going to learn anything in school, he might as well make the most of his time there.

He often threatened to beat Rawly up, but he never did. Instead, he found other ways to torment him. Charlie would purposely bump into Rawly in the hallways, causing him to drop an armload of books. Or he'd shoot spitballs through a straw at the back of Rawly's head during lunchtime.

One day Charlie snatched an *Avengers* comic book away from Rawly and strolled down the hall without saying a word. When Rawly yelled at him to give it back, Charlie Matuszak turned around, waved a fist in the air and said, "Take it from me, punk."

Rawly stood rigid with fear. Charlie was twice his size. He watched helplessly as Charlie walked away with the comic book.

Then he heard a voice say, "Don't worry, dude. I'll take care of him for you."

Rawly turned and saw a tall, lanky kid he recognized from his science class. His name was Devin or Nathan. The kid had long, spindly arms that Charlie Matuszak could easily snap in half, like chicken bones.

Rawly snorted. "What are you going to do? Beat him up for me?"

"Do not despair, my friend," the kid said. "For the pen is mightier than the sword."

Rawly didn't understand what the kid meant. But then, Devin or Nathan was always saying weird stuff like that in class.

Two days later, Charlie Matuszak was absent from school. No surprise there. Rawly figured Charlie was probably cutting classes or something. When Charlie didn't show up the next day or the Monday of the following week, Rawly began to hope that maybe Charlie had transferred to another school.

No such luck.

Charlie walked into class on Tuesday morning, looking strangely dispirited, as if his dog had just died. Charlie's expression turned to rage when he sat down and found a note inside his desk that read: YOU HAVE BEEN WARNED. NOW LEAVE MY FRIENDS ALONE. OR ELSE!!!

When class was over, Charlie grabbed Rawly by his shirt and slammed him against the lockers. He demanded that Rawly tell him about the dirty magazines. Quaking with fear, Rawly sputtered that he didn't know anything about any dirty magazines. Charlie could sense that Rawly was telling the truth, so he let him go.

That afternoon, the kid Rawly now knew as Nevin Steinberg explained Charlie Matuszak's absences. It seemed that Mr. and Mrs. Matuszak had received a letter from the school informing them that their son was being given a three-day suspension, after a custodian found a stack of porn magazines in Charlie's locker. Both the letter and the envelope had the official school district logo and the principal's signature.

Nevin figured Charlie's parents couldn't be any brighter than their dim-witted son. Sure enough, neither parent showed up to contest the suspension, despite Charlie's protests that he'd never had any dirty magazines in his locker.

Soon after that, Charlie Matuszak received a coupon in the mail for five free pizzas and drinks from Gino's Pizzeria as part of a "Getting to Know Our Neighbors" promotion. Charlie wasn't about to share his prize with his parents or his two snotty little brothers. Anyway, the letter was addressed to him. He could invite whoever he wanted. He decided to treat three other grunts from his school instead.

After they'd had their fill of pizzas and sodas, Charlie, grinning like a chimpanzee, handed the cashier the coupon.

Three minutes later, Mr. and Mrs. Matuszak got a call from the manager of Gino's Pizzeria, telling them that their son and his friends had eaten sixty-five dollars worth of pizzas and drinks and had tried to pay for them with a counterfeit coupon.

The next morning, Charlie found a note taped to his locker that said: THIS IS YOUR SECOND WARNING. DON'T PIZZA ME OFF. LEAVE MY FRIENDS ALONE. OR ELSE!!!

Charlie Matuszak didn't bother Rawly after that. Rawly didn't know if it was because Charlie had been frightened off by Nevin's pranks, or if Charlie had become so obsessed with finding out who was setting him up that he didn't have time to waste on small fish like him.

That was two years ago.

Since then, Rawly and Nevin's friendship had been hit-or-miss. Sometimes, they were as close as brothers. Rawly had met Nevin around the time of Jaime's accident. Nevin was the only person Rawly trusted to tell about what had happened to Jaime. Other times, Nevin acted so clownish, Rawly couldn't discuss anything serious with him.

The bus stopped. The doors hissed open and a woman holding two grocery bags got on. Rawly looked out the window and saw a Walmart.

But the Walmart was five miles past his exit! Rawly had lost track of where he was going.

As the doors started to shut, Rawly ran to the front of the bus. "Sorry, I need to get off."

The driver opened the doors and let him out.

Rawly stood in front of the Walmart and looked around. The bus had been traveling south. It made sense to him that in order to get to the restaurant he would have to catch a bus going north.

He crossed the street and walked toward the bus stop in front of Winnetka Creek.

Because of the persistent heavy storms, the water in Winnetka Creek had risen to an unusually high level. Any more rain and it would begin to spill into the streets.

A Channel 12 News truck was parked along the curb. In the distance, Rawly saw Delia Franco, the Channel 12 newswoman who had done the report about the pig. She was standing near the steel and timber bridge that stretched across the water. Apparently she was doing a story about the potential flood threat.

The reporter, wearing a yellow rain slicker, spoke into her microphone and pointed to the high, rushing water, which almost touched the bottom of the bridge, while a cameraman videotaped her.

Rawly decided to stay away from the reporter. When the pig story aired, his mother cursed Delia Franco and her news coverage. From then on, she refused to watch the Channel 12 News.

As Rawly reached the bus stop, he was startled by the sound of loud, screeching tires. A white Mercedes Benz skidded uncontrollably on the wet street. It slid sideways, then forward, but it didn't slow down. It continued accelerating at a high rate of speed.

Rawly turned.

The car was coming at him!

CHAPTER FOURTEEN

Rawly jumped out of the way. The car hit the curb at the edge of Winnetka Creek and vaulted over it, missing him by inches. It tore across the grass, flew past the embankment and plunged into the swollen waters below.

Rawly ran to the edge of the creek. The car sat at a tilt, halfway submerged. The airbags had deployed. He saw someone inside, a female, struggling to remove her seatbelt. Finally she managed to undo the buckle. She pulled on the door handle, but the strong waters jammed the door shut. The car began to fill with water.

Rawly looked all around, wild-eyed. His heart pumped spasmodically. He wanted to jump into the creek to help the woman, but he realized it wouldn't do any good. He wasn't a swimmer. His only swimming experience had come from swimming at Hurricane Harbor. But the water park consisted mostly of slides and lazy rivers, and the main pool was too crowded for anyone to do any real swimming.

Rawly saw the woman floating inside, thrashing her arms and legs, screaming. He was aware that he was watching her drown.

"Hey!" Rawly shouted at Delia Franco and the cameraman. "There's a woman trapped inside that car!"

The reporter, holding her microphone in front of her face, ran toward him. The cameraman trailed after her, keeping his camera aimed at the car.

Rawly returned his attention to the woman. She had flipped herself upside down and was kicking at her car's sunroof.

Seconds later, the glass panel shattered. The woman pushed her head out of the hole like a jack-in-the-box and sucked in a deep breath of air.

She was a lot younger than Rawly first thought, probably no older than Jaime.

The woman pulled herself up and sat on the roof. Her eyes were glazed. Blood poured out of her nose and from a gash that had opened up above her left eyebrow. Her dark-brown hair hung down her face like snakes.

Rawly cupped his hands around his mouth and shouted, "Are you all right?"

His voice snapped the woman out of her disoriented state. She looked at Rawly and nodded weakly. She reached back inside the car, grabbed her purse and took out her cell phone.

Delia Franco and the cameraman stood next to Rawly. The reporter continued speaking into her microphone while the cameraman captured the scene on tape.

All of a sudden, the car lurched to one side. The muddy creek bed that had initially supported it gave way, and the car sank, leaving the woman floating in the water. Immediately, the raging currents swept her away.

Delia Franco and the cameraman ran after her, continuing to report what they were witnessing.

Rawly chased after them. He could see the woman's head bobbing up and down as the water carried her off.

In desperation, the woman grabbed a tree branch that floated alongside her, but the branch couldn't support her weight. Rawly watched her sink into the water. She burst through the surface a moment later, gasping for air.

He had to do something. But what?

Think like Batman, Nevin said in his mind. *You're in a predicament. You've got a problem to solve. Go over all your options.*

Rawly's eyes darted around maniacally for an answer. A branch? A vine? What could he use to rescue her?

Up ahead, he saw the steel and timber bridge.

That's it!

He had only one chance. If he failed, the woman was sure to drown.

Still running, Rawly ripped open his long-sleeve blue shirt. The white buttons popped off it like bullets. He pulled off the shirt and raced to the middle of the bridge. He dropped to his stomach and stretched himself through a pair of steel beams that formed an X on the side. He got as close as he could to the edge of the bridge and dangled his shirt.

As the woman drifted toward him, he shouted, "Grab it!"

Even in her panicked state, the woman had enough composure to understand what Rawly was doing. She lunged up and grasped the shirt sleeve with both hands.

The sudden weight almost jerked Rawly off the bridge. He was dragged forward. Splinters from the wooden floor stabbed his chest and stomach. Ignoring the pain, Rawly turned himself sideways and locked his legs around the X beams.

"Don't let me fall!" the woman screamed. "God, don't let me fall!"

Rawly tried to pull her up, but he didn't have the leverage he needed to lift her.

The woman kicked her legs and tried to swing herself to the top.

"Stop moving!" Rawly yelled. "You're going to tear the . . . "

R-r-i-i-p.

The woman shrieked.

Rawly reached down as far as he could and grabbed her by the back of her pants. With his legs still coiled around the steel beams, he yanked her up as hard as he could.

Coughing and spitting creek water, the woman scrambled up Rawly's arms and climbed over him. She squeezed through the steel beams and pulled herself to the floor, where she collapsed, face down.

Rawly hauled himself up and crawled toward her on all fours.

Delia Franco and the cameraman hovered over them. A small crowd of witnesses, who had seen the car hydroplaning, gathered nearby.

"Is she all right?" the reporter asked.

"I don't know." Rawly gently turned the woman over and stared at her ashen face. He thought he should perform CPR, but the only thing he knew about CPR was that you covered the other person's mouth with yours and blew into it.

He shifted his body and leaned into the woman. He held her face in his hands and awkwardly pressed his mouth against hers. He puffed a couple of breaths of air into her, and then he stopped. What if he was doing it wrong? What if he was causing the woman more harm than good? He looked up at the people standing around them—three Walmart employees, an elderly woman with her young granddaughter, and a teenage girl wearing a Dallas Mavericks jersey.

Rawly reached in his pocket and pulled out his cell phone. One of the Walmart workers, an old man with a blue bib apron, told Rawly that he had already called 9-1-1. "Me, too," the teenage girl said. She showed Rawly her cell phone.

The little girl looked up at her grandmother and asked, "Nana, is the lady dead?"

At that moment, the woman began to stir. Rawly took her by the shoulders and said, "Don't try to get up. Someone's already called for help."

Soon he heard a faint *woowoowoowoo*. As the sound grew louder, Rawly saw an ambulance approaching, its red, white and blue lights flashing.

The ambulance stopped at the curb of Winnetka Creek, and two paramedics jumped out. They pulled a gurney from the back and wheeled it toward them. After making a quick assessment of the situation, one of the paramedics clamped an oxygen mask over the woman's mouth while the other one took down a report. Afterwards, they lifted her onto the gurney. As they rolled her into the ambulance, the woman took Rawly's hand. She offered a slight smile and said haltingly, "Thank you . . . for saving . . . my life."

Because of all the commotion, Rawly hadn't had a chance to think about what he had done.

"That was the most amazing thing I've ever seen," the cameraman told him. "She would've drowned if it wasn't for you. You're a hero, kid. An honest to goodness hero. And the best part is that I caught the whole thing on tape."

A police officer arrived a few minutes later. Both the officer and Delia Franco asked Rawly a million questions, but their words sounded distant, muted. Rawly's mind raced back to the start of the incident—the car driving out of control, almost striking him; the car plunging into the water; the woman scrambling to free herself from her watery prison; escaping, only to fall into the creek and be swept away in the heavy currents; Rawly throwing himself down on the bridge floor and using his shirt to fish the woman out of the water.

Thank you . . . for saving . . . my life.

You're a hero, kid. An honest to goodness hero.

An hour later, Rawly, exhausted, dragged himself inside the restaurant.

His mother stared at him with cold speculation. "Do you have any idea what time it is? You've had me worried sick. I called the school. I talked to Jennifer Steinberg. I even sent Teresita to the comic book store to see if you were in there. I was getting ready to get in the car to try to find you. And look at you. You're all dirty."

"I . . . I . . . " Rawly started. His knees buckled. Then he passed out.

CHAPTER FIFTEEN

Rawly regained consciousness a few moments later. He was lying on the couch in the restaurant office with a wet towel on his forehead. His mother stood over him, fanning his face with a menu.

"What happened?" Rawly asked.

"You tell me," his mother answered in a harsh tone. "You were late for work. Then you fainted." Her eyes narrowed with suspicion. "You're not doing anything you're not supposed to, are you?"

Rawly removed the towel and sat up. "No, Mom. Wait! Are you accusing me of . . . "

"I'm not accusing you of anything. But you don't have a fever. You don't look sick and . . . where's your shirt?"

"Mom, I saved a lady's life," Rawly blurted out. "She lost control of her car and drove into Winnetka Creek."

"Winnetka Creek? What were you doing way over there?"

Rawly told her everything.

When he finished, his mother weighed his story with mixed feelings. She cracked her knuckles and said, "Rawly, I know you were trying to do the right thing, but you almost got yourself killed. You could've drowned trying to save that woman. You should've let the police or the paramedics rescue her. That's their job."

Rawly gawked at her in disbelief. "Mom, don't you understand? She was drowning! The police and the paramedics hadn't arrived yet. There was no one else who could help her."

She cracked her knuckles again. "I know. It's just that after what happened to Jaime . . . Rawly, I can't lose you, too."

"Mom, I'm fine. I think it was all that excitement that got to me, but I'm okay."

"So who was this woman you saved?" she asked, changing her tone. "Did you get her name?"

"Yeah, her name's Nicolette Demetrius."

"Demetrius?" Rawly's mother ran the name through her mind. "Not of the diamond jeweler's Demetrius family, is she?"

"I don't know. I remembered her name because she said it several times—to the cop, to the paramedics and to the reporter. Oh, yeah, there's going to be a story about me on the Channel 12 ten o'clock news."

"Channel 12?" The words made Rawly's mother cringe.

While Rawly rested, his mother opened a cabinet door and took out a red and yellow T-shirt for him to wear. The shirt, which bore the restaurant's logo, was left over from a promotion she had held several years ago. Rawly had left his blue shirt at Winnetka Creek, and his T-shirt was ripped and smeared with mud.

After his mother went back to work, Rawly called Nevin. He hoped Nevin wouldn't be mad after the way he had treated him at school.

"Dude, are you telling me you saved Nikki Demetrius's life?"

"She said her name was Nicolette."

"No, dude. It's Nikki. Don't you know who she is?"

"No."

"Wait a minute. What does she look like?"

Rawly described her.

"Dude, what planet have you been living on?" Nevin asked. "Nikki Demetrius is a famous fashion model. Her face is always on the covers of those girl magazines."

Rawly chuckled. "How would you know what's in those magazines? Is that the kind of stuff you read?"

"No, but my mom and my sister do. I'll bet you a dollar it's her."

"I don't think it's the same person," Rawly said. "I mean, this woman was kind of pretty, but she didn't look like a model."

"Of course she didn't," Nevin said, "not with her nearly drowning and bleeding and stuff. But how many women are there named Nikki Demetrius?"

"She called herself Nicolette," Rawly said, still unconvinced they were talking about the same person. "Look, I've got to go. I'll see you at school tomorrow."

After the restaurant closed, Rawly and his mother and all the restaurant employees gathered around the television set that hung behind what used to be the bar and watched the Channel 12 News.

Brent Edwards, the evening anchorman, opened the broadcast with Rawly's rescue story. Beside him was a superimposed double-panel screen. The left side of the screen had a picture of the late actor, Christopher Reeve, as Clark Kent, running, ripping open his white shirt and revealing his blue Superman costume underneath. The opposite panel showed Rawly Sánchez, running, ripping open his blue shirt and revealing his white T-shirt underneath.

"Hey, look at that," Fredo said. "It's Rawly."

Rawly's mouth fell open. He couldn't believe it. He looked like a superhero!

"A daring and dramatic rescue took place earlier today after a white Mercedes Benz skidded off the road at the intersection of Dryer and Bellmonte and plunged into the rising waters of Winnetka Creek in Oak Cliff," the anchorman reported. "Did I say a daring and dramatic rescue?" He flashed a toothy grin. "Let's call it a super one. Here's Delia Franco to explain."

When Delia Franco's face appeared on TV, the restaurant workers booed.

"Shh! I want to hear," Mrs. Sánchez said.

"Rawly Sánchez, a fourteen-year-old ninth grader at North Oak Cliff High School is being hailed a hero after his quick-thinking and fast actions saved famed fashion model, Nikki Demetrius, from drowning," Delia Franco reported.

Nevin was right. Her name *was* Nikki.

The restaurant workers cheered and clapped. Mrs. Sánchez chewed her nails as she listened.

"At around four-thirty this afternoon, twenty-two year old Nikki Demetrius, the daughter of diamond magnate, Andrei Demetrius, lost control of her car after her brakes locked when she tried to stop at a red light. Her car sideslipped off the road and plummeted into Winnetka Creek. Miraculously, Ms. Demetrius survived her fall. Let's take a look at this incredible footage."

The news aired a video clip of the accident.

"As you can see, Ms. Demetrius managed to pull herself from her car," Delia Franco said. "However, the soft soil in the creek bed gave way, and her car sank into the water. What happened next can only be described, as Brent told you, *super*."

The next clip showed Rawly, ripping open his shirt, as he ran after Nikki Demetrius. The camera captured him dropping to his stomach on the bridge floor, hanging his shirt over and pulling the fashion model out of the water.

Mrs. Sánchez gasped when she saw Rawly almost yanked into the creek.

"The word hero tends to be overused these days, but this is one time when it is truly deserved," Delia Franco said as she concluded her report. "Nikki Demetrius was taken to Methodist Medical Center for injuries she suffered in the accident, but she is expected to fully recover. This is Delia Franco reporting for Channel 12 News."

"Wow!" Teresita cried. "I've never seen anything like that in my whole life." She kissed Rawly on the cheek.

Fredo patted him on the back and shook his hand. "We've got ourselves a real live hero here."

"So it *was* a Demetrius family member," Rawly's mother said. "They're one of the richest families in Texas, you know."

"Do you think they'll give Rawly a reward?" Isabel asked.

"They should," Fredo said. "I mean, he saved Andrei Demetrius's daughter. How much do you think her life's worth?"

"*Mucho dinero*," Enrique, one of the assistant cooks answered. He pretended to rub dollar bills between his fingers. "*Mucho, mucho dinero*." He smiled, revealing two gold upper teeth.

Rawly's mother mused over Enrique's words. She started to comment on them but changed her mind. "Come on. Let's get the place cleaned up so we can go home."

"You're not going to make Rawly clean up, too, are you?" Fredo asked, smiling. "I mean, he's a hero. Heroes shouldn't have to sweep floors."

"I don't mind," Rawly said. "I should do my job like everyone else."

"Spoken like a true hero," Teresita said and handed him a broom.

CHAPTER SIXTEEN

The following morning, Rawly walked outside his house and picked up a copy of *The Dallas Morning News* from the front lawn. He liked to read the comics section before he left for school. This time he didn't make it to the comics.

On the front page of the paper was a large picture of the double-panel photo that had been shown on the news the night before, with Rawly, side by side, with Christopher Reeve. Above the picture, in bold letters, was the caption: SIMPLY SUPER! The article told almost the exact story that had aired on TV.

Rawly ran to his mother's bedroom and pounded on the door.

Her slurry voice invited him in.

"Mom, look!" He jumped on the bed next to her like he used to when he was little and held the newspaper in front of her face.

She sat up, pulling her blanket to her neck. She squinted, trying to make out the blurry image on the newspaper. "Get me my glasses."

Rawly picked up her reading glasses from the nightstand and handed them to her. "Isn't this cool?"

Her face beamed with pride as she read the article. She stared at the photograph and said, "Finally, someone in this family did something right."

Rawly understood what she meant. Jaime's picture had once been in the newspaper, too. Above his picture, though, were the words: DRUNK DRIVER KILLS METHODIST HOSPITAL NURSE.

"This is nice," Rawly's mother said. "Real nice." She returned to the part in the story that briefly detailed the Demetrius family's background. She thought about what Enrique had said. *Mucho dinero. Mucho, mucho dinero.*

"I'm going to take this to the restaurant to show everyone," she said. "Then I'll buy a frame for it and hang it there."

Rawly had wanted to take the newspaper to school to show the guys. Maybe he could buy another copy later.

As it turned out, he didn't need the newspaper.

When he got on the school bus, he was greeted with whistles, cheers and applause. Jennifer Barclay had brought a copy of *The Dallas Morning News* and had been passing it around to everyone.

Miss Olivia, the bus driver, grinned a piano mouth of teeth. "There's my hero," she said and gave Rawly a hug. "When I saw you on the news last night, I told my mother, 'That boy rides on my bus. I know him.'"

"What's it feel like to be a hero?" Santiago Pérez asked him.

Jennifer Barclay held up the newspaper and said, "Simply super! Right, Rawly?"

Arlie Hoyle giggled like a little girl. "Hey, Rawly, what was it like to kiss Nikki Demetrius?"

Rawly's face turned red. "I didn't kiss her."

"Sure you did," Arlie said. "They had a close-up of you and Nikki on TV last night. You were practically playing tonsil hockey with her."

"I was trying to give her mouth-to-mouth," Rawly answered defensively.

Arlie hee-heed again. "You sure were. And you gave it to her, man. Right on the mouth."

"I wish Nikki Demetrius would give *me* mouth-to-mouth," Santiago said dreamily.

The reception Rawly received when he got on the bus was nothing compared to what awaited him when he arrived at school. A swarm of reporters and photographers rushed the bus as soon as it pulled up in front of the school. Microphones were shoved in Rawly's face. TV news cameras zoomed in on him, and bulbs flashed like fireworks. Strangers he had never met called him by name and fired a barrage of questions.

"What was going through your mind when you saw the car go into the water?"

"How does it feel knowing you saved someone's life?"

"Where did you learn CPR?"

"Did you know it was Nikki Demetrius when you pulled her out of the water?"

Questions came at such a rapid pace that Rawly's mind couldn't process them fast enough. The crowds came closer. Noisier. Rowdier. Suffocating him.

Rawly stood flabbergasted. He was aware that he had rescued someone important, but it hadn't dawned on him how big a name Nikki Demetrius was. As of yesterday, he had never even heard of her.

Finally, Mr. Hair pushed his way though the crowd. He wrapped an arm around Rawly and raised a hand to signal silence. He announced to the press that he, the teachers, the staff and the students at North Oak Cliff High School were all proud of Rawly, and that Rawly had brought great honor to the school and to the city. The photographers clicked their cameras while Mr. Hair smiled with an arm clamped around Rawly's shoulders.

Rawly looked at the walls of people that surrounded him. His heart swelled. Yesterday, he had been the laughing stock of the school. Twenty-four hours later, he was a star. In one day, he had gone from zero to hero.

The questions continued coming at him in loud, sometimes inaudible, murmurs. Rawly smiled at the reporters and did his best to answer their questions.

After a few more pictures, Mr. Hair reminded the reporters that school was still in session. Then he escorted Rawly to the building.

Nevin hurried up to them. "I'll take it from here, sir," he told Mr. Hair. "I'll make sure Rawly makes it to his classes all right." Nevin pushed back crowds of students. "Step aside, step aside," he ordered. "My client cannot be bothered at the moment. He has classes to attend. However, if you wish to speak with him, you may make an appointment with me, and I'll try to fit you into his schedule."

Miyoko ran up to them with a look of rapture in her eyes. "Rawly, is it true what the kids are saying? That you saved Nikki Demetrius's life?"

Rawly stiffened in apprehension. "Um, listen, Miyoko, about the other night. I'm sorry I broke your guitar. I didn't mean to. It's just . . . "

Miyoko waved off his concern. "Don't worry about that. Tell me what happened with Nikki."

Rawly gave her a brief version of the story he had told a dozen times.

"That is so awesome!" she cried. "What was Nikki like? Did you get a chance to talk to her?"

"Not really. She was pretty much out of it."

"But she did say something to you, dude," Nevin said. "Tell Miyoko what Nikki told you."

"She said, 'Thank you for saving my life.'"

Nevin grinned. "Is that cool or what? Nikki Demetrius said that to him. She knows Rawly saved her."

"Are you going to get to meet her?" Miyoko asked.

"I don't know."

"Of course he is," Nevin said. "Surely Nikki Demetrius wants to meet the guy who saved her life."

"If you get a chance to see her, can I go with you?" Miyoko asked, her eyes brimming with hope. "I would absolutely die for a chance to meet Nikki."

Rawly couldn't believe it. Miyoko was practically begging him to take her to meet Nikki Demetrius. She wasn't even mad that he had broken her guitar. "Sure, I guess," he said. It was the least he could do.

Nevin rested an arm on Rawly's shoulder. "We'll all go. The more, the merrier, I always say."

Miyoko brushed back her hair. "I've always dreamed of being a model, just like Nikki. Maybe if I get to talk to her, she can tell me how to get started."

During English class, Ms. Palacios had Rawly stand in front of the class. She held up a copy of *The Dallas Morning News* story and congratulated him for his bravery.

After Rawly sat down, Ms. Palacios said, "William Shakespeare wrote, *Some men are born great. Some achieve greatness, and some have greatness thrust upon them.*"

She asked the class what they thought Shakespeare meant. Most of the responses centered on Rawly saving the fashion model's life. Afterwards, Ms. Palacios had her students write an essay about what makes a hero.

Rawly thought about how Sid Lundy had described the qualities of a hero: courage, sacrificing oneself for the good of others, being able to overcome adversity. In one way or another, yesterday, he had met all those qualifications.

Throughout the day, kids commented on his rescue.

"Hi, Superman."

"Look! Up in the sky! It's a bird. It's plane. No, it's Super Rawly!"

Iris Solís caught up with him in the hallway and wrapped her arms around his neck. "See, Rawly? I told you, you were smart. You only had seconds to think, but you knew exactly what to do."

Rawly gently peeled her arms off. He looked around to see if Arlie or one of the other guys was watching. "Yeah, uh, thanks."

During lunch, Falesha Coe and Lisa Kirksey pointed at him and sang and danced to Aretha Franklin's, *Rescue Me.*

> . . . *Come on and rescue me*
> *come on, baby and rescue me*
> *come on, baby and rescue me*
> *'coz I need you by my side*
> *can't you see that I'm lonely*
> *Rescue me.*

That was fine. Rawly didn't mind. It was certainly better than having to endure another stupid gorilla joke. He gave them a "thumbs up."

Rawly had never had a better day. Even algebra class wasn't bad. Like most of the other teachers, Mr. Mondragón had hung up the newspaper article. He praised Rawly on his courage and quick-thinking.

"Now let's see if you can apply that same quick-thinking to this," Mr. Mondragón added with a wink. He turned on the projector and showed the class a set of word problems. They were instructed to write an algebraic equation for each one.

1. Marco has a collection of candies that include Jolly Ranchers, Atomic Fireballs and Starbursts. He has twice as many Jolly Ranchers as Atomic Fireballs and three more Starbursts than Jolly Ranchers. He has a total of 28 pieces of candy. How many Fireballs does Marco have?

Rawly had a problem to solve. He went over all his options. He thought of everything he knew about algebra. He made a few calculations on his paper and . . . bingo! He had an answer.

He read over his work to make sure it was correct. Satisfied, he copied the next problem. He paused and looked up at the newspaper article stapled on the bulletin board. Suddenly he felt invigorated, energized. He wrote a few figures on his paper, then smiled as the answer came to him.

Bring it on, Mr. Mondragón, he thought, and jotted down the next problem. Bring it on!

CHAPTER SEVENTEEN

Mrs. Sánchez was sitting in her office, talking on the phone. She looked up when Rawly walked in and motioned for him to sit down. Rawly tossed his backpack on the floor and relaxed on the couch.

As soon as she got off the phone, Rawly's mother pointed to her computer and said excitedly, "Rawly, look at this."

He rose and came around her desk.

"We've received tons of emails from people asking about you." She scrolled down a long list of names. "I've hardly had a chance to get any work done because I've been on the phone. Your *tíos* and *tías*, your *güelos*—everyone's been calling." Her eyes glinted with delight. "Not only that, but guess what? We've gotten calls from all the news stations. They want to interview you."

"Yeah, they showed up at my school, too," Rawly told her.

His mother rolled her eyes and let out an exaggerated sigh, trying to look annoyed. "Oh, and that Delia Franco from Channel 12 News called, too. I suppose we'll have to let her interview you again since her station covered the story first. She wants to come by the restaurant tonight."

Rawly thought back to Open Mic Night and how he had made a fool of himself. There had been about a hundred-fifty people in the auditorium then. If he appeared on television, who knew how many viewers would be watching?

"Mom, I don't know if I want to be on TV," he said.

"Why not?"

Rawly wet his lips. "Because . . . what if I mess up? What if I say the wrong things? It'll be so embarrassing."

"You'll do fine," his mother said. "Anyway, I don't know why you would be nervous. You were on the news last night."

"Yeah, but that was different," Rawly said. "I started talking to the reporter before I had a chance to think about what I wanted to say."

Rawly's mother opened an email from the Dallas Tortilla Factory and skimmed its message. "I wouldn't worry about it. Just tell the reporters your story, the way you told it to me. The way you told it yesterday."

She clicked off the Internet and gave Rawly her full attention. "I also got a call from a man who said he was a representative of the Demetrius family. He told me that as soon as Nikki Demetrius is feeling better, she wants meet you."

Rawly's anxiety eased for a moment. Miyoko wanted to go with him to see Nikki Demetrius. This would be the perfect opportunity.

"But I still haven't told you the best news." Mrs. Sánchez wrapped an arm around Rawly's waist and drew him close. "Tomorrow morning, the TV cameras for *ABC Good Day America* will be here. You're going to take part in a live teleconference interview. I told them it would be okay since you don't have school tomorrow. Then after

that, you'll be appearing on the *Today* show. They'll get
here after the *ABC* people leave. And after that . . . "

Rawly's eyebrows shot up. "Whoa, Mom. What?"

"That's right. You're going to be on national TV tomorrow. Isn't that exciting?"

Rawly didn't think it was exciting at all.

The day after the Cinco de Mayo program, Mr. Dibbles invited the participants to watch the video of their performance. The kids giggled when Rawly was shown on the screen, standing like a zombie, ringing the church bell. They howled with laughter when the façade fell on top of him.

It was one thing to be interviewed on the local news, but what would it be like knowing that the whole country was watching him? Rawly could picture himself staring at the camera with that same living-dead look in his eyes, while the hosts of those morning shows fired questions at him about the accident.

"Why didn't you ask me first before volunteering me to be on all those news shows?" he asked curtly.

"I'm sorry, Rawly. It's just that everything happened so fast. They wanted an answer right away, so I said yes."

"But Nevin and I are supposed to go to the fair tomorrow."

Friday was Secondary Schools Fair Day in Dallas. Students and teachers had received free tickets to attend the State Fair of Texas, and all middle and high schools would be closed.

His mother's warm manner disappeared. "You can go to the fair any time," she said. "Right now, the interviews are more important. Think of all the attention your television appearances will bring to the restaurant." She opened the office door. "Go to the kitchen and tell Fredo to fix you a plate. Then as soon as you finish eating, I'll drive you home so you can change."

"Change? For what?"

"For your interview with Delia Franco."

"But you don't even like the Channel 12 News."

"It doesn't matter. It'll be free publicity for the restaurant. I'll call the other news stations and have them come after Channel 12 finishes." His mother nudged him out the door. "Now go eat. I'm going to look for that banner we used to have hanging outside. I want to put it up where it can be seen when the cameras are on you."

Shortly before seven o'clock, the Channel 12 News truck pulled up in front of the restaurant. Rawly's mother met Delia Franco and a cameraman at the door. The reporter apologized once again for the pig story. She had already told Rawly's mother over the phone how sorry she was. "Please understand that it was an assignment, Mrs. Sánchez. I have to do what my boss says."

Rawly's mother took them to the room that used to be the bar. Behind the counter hung a red vinyl banner with the words LA CHICHEN-ITZA MEXICAN RESTAURANT in yellow letters.

Rawly came in and greeted the guests.

While the cameraman set up his equipment, Delia Franco and Rawly sat down on barstools and waited. Rawly's mother stood behind the cameraman to make sure the banner could be seen clearly.

Rawly fidgeted in his chair. He crossed and uncrossed his legs. He tugged at the tie his mother had made him wear.

He recalled what Ms. Coleman had told the participants on Open Mic Nite. "The audience came to see a good show. Let's give them one. Remember, they're all rooting for you. If you mess up, don't stop. Just keep going."

But he hadn't kept going at Open Mic Nite. After he fell on top of Miyoko, he ran out of the auditorium like a coward.

A *steenkin'* coward.

God, please don't let me mess up, Rawly prayed in his mind.

Delia Franco started with simple questions. She wanted to know how Rawly liked school. He said he liked it fine, except for algebra. She asked if he had any hobbies. He told her about his comic book collection. Rawly hoped he didn't come off sounding like a geek.

She asked about his family. Without elaborating, Rawly told her he had an older brother who lived out of town.

From time to time, curious customers stole peeks in the bar, but Rawly's mother shooed them away.

When the interview was over, Delia Franco shook Rawly's hand. She told him he had done a terrific job, and that a clip of the interview would air during the ten o'clock broadcast.

Rawly rose from his barstool on wobbly legs. His armpits were leaking sweat. His heart was racing. He took a couple of deep breaths to steady himself. He didn't care if he had done a terrific job. He just hoped he didn't look like a complete idiot on TV.

The other local news stations arrived later, at staggered times. By the third interview, Rawly, much more relaxed, comfortably related his story.

After work, Rawly and his mother stopped by a 7-Eleven to buy extra newspapers. When they got home, Rawly cut out his article and thumb-tacked it to the cork bulletin board above the desk in his bedroom. He stared at his superhero figurines that stood on his dresser. Superman was there. So were Batman, Daredevil, the Flash, Green Arrow, Spider-Man and Wolverine. His eyes darted from his newspaper photo, then back to his toys.

"You guys and I have something in common," Rawly said aloud and smiled.

CHAPTER EIGHTEEN

Rawly told his story on *ABC Good Day America* and the *Today* show. He repeated it in Spanish to a reporter from Telemundo. It was back to speaking in English when he appeared on CNN.

The night before, he watched his interviews on the local news. He studied his facial expressions and body language. He noticed he blinked a lot. Several times he chewed his nails. During his first interview, he hunched over on his barstool like an old man. His mother stood in front of him and bounced her hands, palms up, urging him to straighten. He thought she was telling him to speak louder, so he did.

Rawly fixed those mistakes when he appeared on national TV. He still didn't like speaking in front of the cameras, but he would have to get used to it.

After all, he was a hero.

The tabloid and entertainment news programs had been running stories about Nikki Demetrius's accident. They aired pictures of Rawly, which had been taken at his school, as well as the clip of him rescuing the fashion model.

On Saturday morning, algebra tutoring went especially well. Many of the terms that had escaped Rawly's

understanding—integers, monomials, binomials, polyno-
mials—were finally starting to make sense.

Mr. Mondragón told the class that he had seen Rawly
on the news. He asked if anyone else had seen him, but
no one answered. Rawly figured that most of the flunkies
who were in tutoring with him didn't spend a lot of time
watching the news.

Class ended a half hour early. Mr. Mondragón, wearing
a burnt orange University of Texas sweatshirt, announced
to the class that he had tickets to the Texas/OU football
game, and he didn't want to be late to it.

Rawly considered dropping by Nevin's house. He wanted to tell him about his interviews, but it probably wasn't a
good time. It was Miriam's wedding day. Rawly figured
things at Nevin's house were pretty hectic. They didn't need
him getting in the way. Besides, Rawly thought Nevin might
be sore at him because he hadn't been able to go to the fair
with him on Friday. Rawly had told Nevin to find some
other guys to go with, but Nevin ignored the suggestion.

"Rawly!" Miyoko ran down the school steps. "Have
you heard from Nikki Demetrius yet?"

"Sort of," Rawly said. "A representative from her family called to say that Nikki wants to meet me as soon as
she's better."

"Really?" Miyoko squealed. "You will take me to see
her, won't you?"

Rawly's face lit up. "Sure."

"By the way, you looked great on TV."

Rawly grinned. "You saw me? Why didn't you tell Mr.
Mondragón?"

Miyoko tossed back her long hair and turned up her
nose. "I don't say anything to that stupid man if I don't
have to."

Miyoko's words stung him. Rawly didn't particularly care for Mr. Mondragón, but he never thought of him as being stupid. Even if he did, he would never say it aloud. It was disrespectful to call a teacher that.

"Yesterday morning, I was blow-drying my hair, when my mom burst into my bathroom and started screaming at me like the crazy woman she is," Miyoko said. "I thought she was chewing me out for something, but she was talking about you being on the *Today* show." Miyoko let out a tiny snicker. "I guess she remembered you from Open Mic Nite."

Rawly's face turned red. "Listen, I'm real sorry about . . . "

Miyoko put up a hand to cut him off. "Anyway, she grabbed me by my wrist and dragged me to the den. And there you were, on TV, telling the world about how you saved Nikki Demetrius."

"That was just one interview," Rawly said. "I've done a lot of others."

Miyoko glanced at her watch. Then she looked down the street. "Are you going anywhere right now?" she asked.

"Home, I guess," Rawly said with a shrug.

"Can I . . . I mean . . . want to go get a Coke or something?" Miyoko flashed a dimpled smile. "My treat."

Rawly felt a rush of heat shoot up to his face. He understood what she had said, but his brain was having difficulty fitting her message into the right slot. It occurred to him then why she was making the offer. "You don't have to do that, Miyoko," he said, hardly believing the words that were coming out of his mouth. Still, he didn't want Miyoko to feel obligated to pay him back for taking her to see Nikki Demetrius.

"But I want to," Miyoko said sweetly. "Unless . . . if you have something else to do, I understand."

"No, that would be great!" Rawly said. "We can go to the Jack in the Box across the street. But let me buy."

Miyoko ordered a Diet Coke. Rawly had a strawberry milkshake and an order of fries. He offered her some of his fries, but she declined.

"Too fattening," she said.

Miyoko brought up Nikki Demetrius's name again and the possibility of meeting her idol.

"And I'd like to bring Iris and Amanda, if that's okay. Oh, and I told Melissa and Skye about it, and they want to come, too. But you know, if I invite them, I'll also have to invite Renata and Tracy and Belle. They'll be mad at me if I don't."

Rawly gulped. "Miyoko, I don't think I can invite that many people."

"Sure you can. I mean, you saved Nikki's life. She'll do anything for you."

"I'll see what I can do," Rawly said. "But I can't promise anything." He had no intention of inviting all those girls, but he didn't tell Miyoko that. His dream had finally come true. Here he was at Jack in the Box, having a snack with Miyoko Elena. It was like a date.

"*Teen Vogue* had a story about Nikki Demetrius in last month's issue," Miyoko said. "You know, she models clothes for all the top fashion designers—Marc Jacobs, Vera Wang, Michael Kors, all of them."

Rawly didn't know who those people were, but he nodded as if he understood.

"I once entered this model search contest in *Teen Tropic*, where the winner got a thousand dollars, plus a trip to Hawaii and a chance to appear as a model for a *Teen Tropic* ad campaign," Miyoko said. "I never heard from them, though." She stuck out her lower lip and faked sadness. "My mom doesn't want me to pursue a modeling career because of all the skimpy clothes the girls have to wear. She's so wack. She makes me take back half the clothes I buy. For example, I bought this cute top at Forever 21 to wear to the Jeremy Trio concert, but my mom wouldn't let me wear it because she thought it was too revealing. Do you listen to the Jeremy Trio? They're awesome. I have all their CDs. I think Zac's the cutest of the three, but my friend Skye thinks Doug's cuter."

Rawly tried to follow Miyoko, but he didn't know who or what she was talking about.

"You know, I can't prove it, but I swear my mom's been snooping in my online profile. Like the other day, I wrote that me and Skye and Melissa had skipped school to go see that new movie, *Scarlet Dreams*. The next day, my mom asked me if I wanted her to take me to see *Scarlet Dreams*, knowing full well that I'd already seen it. Then she took away my cell phone because I got that failing notice. She thinks she's punishing me, but really, she's just punishing herself. I mean, how is she going to reach me if there's an emergency? Or what if something happens to me? Then she'll wish she'd never taken away my cell phone."

Rawly realized he wasn't having a conversation with Miyoko. How could he, when she was doing all the talking? He hadn't even gotten a chance to tell her about his interviews. He sipped his milkshake and listened in silence.

"Anyway, I know nothing bad's going to happen to me because I read my horoscope every day. I'm a Sagittarius, you know. Anyway, this morning it said that my life would soon take an upward swing." Her eyes widened.

"Hey, maybe that means . . . " Miyoko stopped when she saw her mother's car pull up in front of the school. "I've got to go. Let me know as soon as you hear something from Nikki, okay?"

"Yeah, I'll . . . " Rawly started, but Miyoko dashed off before he could finish.

He caught the bus home. He wondered if any reporters would be waiting for him. No one was there when he arrived. He checked the time. His mother would be finishing up her visit with Jaime.

Rawly wished he had been able to go to the prison so he could tell Jaime his story in person. He knew Jaime would be so proud of him. Rawly would write and tell him about it. He would also send him a copy of the newspaper article. Jaime couldn't accept anything from visitors, but he could receive mail once it had been inspected.

It was a little past noon. Rawly could still make it to Miriam's wedding if he wanted. The synagogue Nevin's family attended wasn't too far. He could take a quick shower, get dressed, catch the bus, and still get there in plenty of time. The wedding wouldn't start until two o'clock.

He decided against it. He wanted to be home in case someone called to interview him. Anyway, he didn't want to sit through a boring wedding. The only reason Nevin had invited him to go was to keep him company. Rawly was growing tired of feeling like Nevin's side-kick—like Tonto to the Lone Ranger.

I'm not your sidekick, Nevin. I'm nobody's sidekick. I'm a hero!

CHAPTER NINETEEN

Sunday afternoon, Mrs. Steinberg dropped Rawly and Nevin off at the State Fair of Texas. There was no rain in the forecast, but the weather was hot and humid, with temperatures expected to reach the high 80s.

Mrs. Steinberg made Nevin carry an umbrella. "If not for the rain, then for the heat," she said. "You know how easily you sunburn."

The sweltering October air was filled with the enticing scents and sounds of the state fair. People of all ages, sizes and shapes strolled through the grounds. Fairgoers carried stuffed toys they'd won; others munched on yearly fair favorites, like Fletcher's Corny Dogs, Funnel Cakes and Texas Tornado Taters. The Marine band marched in a parade, playing rousing, patriotic music.

Rawly and Nevin made their way past the reflecting pool between the Centennial Building and the Automobile Building, where they were greeted by the fifty-two feet tall, cowboy statue, Big Tex. In a deep Texas drawl, Big Tex welcomed visitors with a warm, "Howdy, folks!"

"Want to get something to eat?" Rawly asked.

"Not yet," Nevin said. "Let's get on a few rides first."

They purchased fair coupons and headed to the Super Midway.

Rawly glanced up at the arched sign at the entrance. Not long ago, Midway used to mean a part of the fair filled with rides and games. Now he also knew it as the name of a small town near Houston, which housed the Ferguson State Prison Farm, where Jaime was locked up.

Rawly and Nevin got on a whirling ride called the Matterhorn. As the ride operator increased the Matterhorn's speed, and the cars surged forward, he teasingly asked the riders, "Do you want to go faster?"

"Yeeeah!" the riders answered euphorically.

Rawly and Nevin raised their arms as the ride zoomed faster and faster on its track. The operator slowed the ride, and then made the cars travel backwards. The wind slapped the riders' faces and whipped their hair. Rawly was glad he and Nevin had gotten on the Matterhorn first, instead of eating. He'd be puking his guts out by now.

Next they rode the Bumper Cars. After that, they rode The Orbiter, a five-arm ride with seats at the end of each arm. The riders spun around in their seats, while being lifted up and down.

When the ride ended, Rawly and Nevin decided to walk off their queasy stomachs.

Rawly wanted to try his skill at the some of the games—the Hoops Toss, the BB Gun Star Shootout or the Dime Throw—but Nevin discouraged him. He told Rawly that even if he did manage to win a large, plush, Sponge Bob Square Pants or a giant Garfield, he would have to lug it around for the rest of the afternoon. And did he really want one of those stuffed toys?

Past the games, they came across a bizarre figure of a man who called himself the Midway Barker. The Midway Barker appeared to be the head and upper body of a man, resting on a pole. He had arms, but the rest of his body below his chest was missing. The Midway Barker joking-ly explained to the crowd that he had been part of a magic trick where he had been sawed in half. Now he couldn't find his other half. He made dumb cracks like, "I'm not half the man I used to be," and "I tried out as a halfback for the Dallas Cowboys, but they cut me."

Rawly and Nevin knew the Midway Barker was an illu-sion, but even as they circled around him, they couldn't figure out the trick.

They left the Midway Barker and made their way to the food concession stands behind the Cotton Bowl. Rawly bought a corny dog. Nevin decided to try the fried guacamole bites.

"How was Miriam's wedding?" Rawly asked.

Nevin dipped a breaded ball of guacamole in ranch dressing and popped it in his mouth. "About as exciting as a snail's race, dude. It lasted forever. And my mom cried the whole time." Nevin pushed the fried guacamole bas-ket in front Rawly. "Taste one. They're pretty good."

Rawly shook his head. "Thanks, but I'll stick to the real stuff we serve at the restaurant." He took another bite of his corny dog.

"I really needed you to be with me at the wedding, Rawls," Nevin said peevishly. "Especially at the recep-tion. You could've rescued me from my uncle Oscar. Uncle Oscar's hitting ninety, and he can't remember a thing. Every ten minutes or so, he'd come up to me and ask, "You been to Monterrey? I've been to Monterrey. Beautiful town, Monterrey."

"Have you been to Monterrey?" Rawly asked.

"No, but Uncle Oscar has. Ask him. He'll be more than happy to tell you all about it." Nevin laughed. "And don't get me started on my aunt Aurelia."

Rawly licked the mustard off his fingers that had dripped from his corny dog. "So what's this guy like that Miriam married? What's his name? David?"

"Yeah. My dad thinks David's a real loser, a *schlemiel*. He doesn't like it that David keeps changing jobs. David says he's trying to move up, but my dad thinks David keeps getting fired from all the places he's worked."

Behind Nevin's shoulder, Rawly saw Cruz Vega and his friends walking toward them. "Come on, Nevin. Let's go."

"But I'm not through eating, dude. What's your hurry?"

"Don't look now, but Cruz Vega and some other goons from Jerks R Us are headed this way."

Cruz and his friends stopped at their table.

"You're the kid from La Chichen-Itza, aren't you?" Cruz asked.

Without looking up, Rawly muttered, "Yeah." He figured Cruz had come by to harass him about the news stories.

"What's your name?" Cruz asked.

Rawly gnawed on the corny dog stick and finished the last remnants of the batter. "Rawly."

Cruz grinned. "Oh, yeah, like the capital of Maryland."

Rawly finally looked up. "No, it's Rawly as in R-A-W-L-Y."

"Saw you on TV, man," Cruz said, now sounding serious. He raised a fist.

Instinctively, Rawly drew back before realizing what Cruz was doing. Rawly smiled nervously. He balled his hand and tapped it against Cruz's.

"That took a lot of guts to do what you did," Cruz said. "Good job, man."

"Yeah, good job," his friends echoed. They banged fists with Rawly, too.

Nevin put up his fist, but no one tapped it. He lowered his hand and said, *"Hola, señores. Me llamo Nevin Steinberg. Soy amigo de Rawly."*

Big Feo scowled at him. "What's your problem, man? You think we don't speak English?"

"No, of course not," Nevin said. "As a matter of fact, you speak it quite well. I was merely trying to converse with you as an *hermano*. That's what Rawly and I are. *Hermanos*. We're Jumex. You know, Jew and . . ."

"You ain't my brother," Big Feo growled. "You ain't even Mexican. Don't call me your brother, *baboso*."

Cruz held him back. *"Cálmate, Juan. Quiero hablar con el otro."* He turned to Rawly and said, "I saw your interview on the Channel 12 News."

"That was my first one," Rawly said proudly. "I've done a bunch more since then."

Cruz sat down. "So, I guess you know that reporter pretty good."

Rawly shrugged. "I wouldn't say we're friends or anything, but . . ."

"And if you asked her to introduce you to the other people on the Channel 12 News, she'd do it. Right?"

Rawly looked at him curiously. "I don't know. Like who?"

"Like the guy who does the sports, Jackhammer Jones," Cruz said.

Nevin balled up his paper napkin and tossed it into the trash barrel. "Yes! Two points!" He smiled at Cruz and said, "Did you know that Jeremiah Jones used to play for the Denver Broncos? He got the nickname 'Jackhammer' because . . ."

"We know," Big Feo said, annoyed.

"I used to play football, you know," Nevin said. "That's how I broke my nose. Listen." He twisted his nose and made a cracking sound with his mouth.

Big Feo pointed a thumb at Nevin and asked, "Who's this clown?"

"Clown?" Nevin said indignantly. "Dudes, I'm on your side." He held up an index finger. "I'm the Bisons' number-one fan. I'm on Cru-u-u-z control, baby! Wooo!"

"¿Quieres ir con nosotros, Rawly?" Cruz asked, ignoring Nevin. "We'll show you how to have a good time."

Big Feo snorted. "It's better than hanging out with this clown."

Rawly looked at Nevin. He thought back to all the times Nevin had dumped him. To the times he had made him look foolish. To the times he had embarrassed him in front of Miyoko. Let's see how Nevin liked being mistreated for a change. Anyway, this was Rawly's chance to be with some real cool guys. Now that he was a hero, he didn't need to hang out with this loser—this *schlemiel.*

He rose from his seat.

Nevin looked at him, confused. "Hey Rawls, where are you going?"

"With them."

Nevin grabbed his umbrella and started to get up.

"Sit down!" Big Feo ordered. "Nobody invited you."

Nevin gave Rawly a pitiful look of appeal.

Rawly smiled shamelessly. "See ya. Wouldn't wanna be ya!" he mocked in a singsong voice before walking off with his new friends.

CHAPTER TWENTY

"**Y**ou're not gonna forget, are you?" Cruz asked.

Rawly opened the passenger door of the front seat of Cruz's car and slid out. He grabbed his stuffed Pink Panther toy from the back. "No, I'll remember."

Cruz flashed an alligator smile. "'Cause we got a deal, right?"

"Right," Rawly answered uncomfortably.

"*Órale*. We'll be talking." Cruz raised his fist and Rawly bumped it with his.

Inside the house, Rawly tossed his Pink Panther toy on the reclining chair and slumped on the couch, exhausted. He had been on his feet for almost nine hours. He slipped off his shoes and socks and rested his legs on the ottoman.

He'd had a great time with Cruz and the other guys —Big Feo, Hector Puentes, Ruben Macías and Eddie Luna. They had gotten on a few rides, including The Slingshot, a ride Nevin had been too chicken to try.

Rawly learned that Eddie Luna was a huge comic book fan. At first, Rawly was skeptical of Eddie's comic book knowledge until Eddie mentioned Eleventh Hour Comics, an independent publishing company that featured quirky titles, such as *The Adventures of Lila Despot and Girdle Boy.* Eddie said he shopped at Heroes & Villains, but Rawly had never seen him there.

The guys all agreed that La Chichen-Itza was the best Mexican restaurant in Dallas, and they told Rawly how lucky he was that his mom owned it.

At the fair, Cruz introduced Rawly to a bunch of girls they ran into. When Cruz told them who Rawly was, the girls mobbed Rawly and asked tons of questions about Nikki Demetrius. A slender, athletic girl named Linda (she pronounced it Leen da), who called Rawly *papi,* made him promise that he would get her an autographed picture of Nikki Demetrius.

Cruz also invited Rawly to a victory party he was hosting Friday night after their game. Cruz called it a victory party because the Bisons were playing the Dallas North Bobcats, a team with a 0 and 7 record, and it was a given that they were going to demolish the Bobcats.

Rawly stretched on the couch and clasped his hands behind his head. He'd had a terrific weekend. *The Dallas Morning News* had written two follow-up stories about him. The TV gossip shows continued to feature stories about Nikki Demetrius's accident, and Rawly had been seen by millions of viewers. He had finally gone out on a date with Miyoko—a short one to Jack in the Box—but a date, nonetheless. He had also made friends with some of North Oak Cliff High's star football players. Rawly had even paid Nevin back for the way he had been treating him.

So why did he feel uneasy, like he had just made a deal with the devil?

The door opened. Rawly's mother walked in and joined him on the couch. Her clothes smelled of Mexican food and tortilla chips.

"How was the fair?" she asked. "Did you and Nevin have fun?"

"It was okay. We, um, got on a few rides, walked around, ate. You know, the usual stuff." Rawly didn't feel he was lying, because that's exactly what he and Nevin had done before they met up with Cruz Vega and his friends.

"I got a call today from Mr. Randall, the spokesperson for the Demetrius family," Rawly's mother said. "He told me that Nikki Demetrius is still recovering from her injuries. She has a separated shoulder, a sprained back, torn ligaments in her ankle and a broken nose. Plus, she had to have stitches for a cut on her forehead."

"Man, that's brutal," Rawly said. "Especially with her being a model and everything."

"Yes, but it could've been worse, you know. A lot worse. If it wasn't for you, that girl would've died." Rawly's mother crossed herself. "And Rawly, you could've died, too."

"But I didn't," Rawly said. "Everything turned out okay."

"The fact is, you risked your life to save hers."

By the tone in his mother's voice, Rawly could tell that she was leading up to something.

"The Demetriuses are very rich, Rawly," she said. "They have diamond stores all over the country, in cities like New York, Chicago, Los Angeles and three here in Dallas." Rawly's mother sat up. "This morning, I Googled Nikki Demetrius's name. Do you know that by the time she was your age, she had made over fifteen million dollars working as a model? Fifteen million dollars!"

Rawly chuckled. "I knew I was in the wrong business. Instead of cleaning tables, I should've been working as a model."

"Rawly, don't laugh," his mother said harshly. "This isn't funny."

"So she's rich. Big deal."

"It *is* a big deal," his mother said. "You saved her life. And you almost got yourself killed doing it. I would say that's worth something, wouldn't you?"

Rawly's smile disappeared. "What are you trying to say, Mom?"

She cracked her knuckles. "Rawly, you know how much we've struggled financially. I try. I try real hard. But I can't ever seem to get ahead. Jaime's accident took just about every penny I had. And I'm not through paying for it. I still get doctor bills and lawyer bills." Her eyes filled with tears. "It's not fair. I didn't ask for any of this. Your daddy's gone, Jaime's gone and I don't have anyone to help me. They owe you, Rawly. The Demetrius family owes you for what you did."

Rawly gasped. "Mom, we can't ask them for money."

Her face hardened. "Why not?"

"Because that would be, I don't know, wrong."

"No, Rawly. It's an answered prayer." His mother gazed across the room at the crucifix hanging above the television. "You don't know how many times I've fallen on my knees at night, praying for a miracle. Rawly, this is it! My prayers have been answered."

Rawly got up from the couch. Sweat trickled down his armpits. "Mom, don't make me do this. I didn't save Nikki Demetrius's life for money. And even if I could charge her, how much would I ask for? A thousand? Ten thousand? A million dollars?"

His mother took his hand and drew him back down. "Everything happens for a reason, Rawly. We've been needing money. Now we have a chance to get out of our financial situation." She removed her blazer and draped it over the Pink Panther stuffed toy. "Mr. Randall wants to know if you'll be available Thursday evening. The Demetrius family wants to thank you personally for what you did, but Nikki's still not in any condition to leave her house. Mr. Randall said he'd send a car to come pick us up."

The tension in Rawly's face eased for a moment. "You mean like in a limo?" He could see himself and Miyoko riding in the back seat of a limousine, being driven to Nikki Demetrius's mansion by a chauffeur.

"I don't know. But that'll be a good time to remind the Demetriuses that their daughter might've died if it wasn't for you. If they have any class, if they have any heart at all, they'll know how to reward you for it."

Rawly didn't like the idea of going to the Demetrius's house, looking like an opportunist, trying to milk them for money. But he did want to take Miyoko to meet Nikki. "Is it okay if I invite a few friends to go with us?" he asked.

"No, it'll just be the two of us. Mr. Randall was very specific. No other visitors. And no cameras. Nikki Demetrius doesn't want the public to see her the way she looks right now."

There went Rawly's chance to score points with Miyoko. He hated to disappoint her. He had already promised to take her.

"When we go, let me do the talking," his mother said. "We need to make sure the Demetriuses understand that you almost lost your life saving that girl's."

Rawly couldn't recall any superheroes who rescued people for money. Granted, some of them, like Batman and Iron Man, were independently wealthy. The Fantastic Four always had plenty of money for Reed Richards's high-tech gadgets. Spider-Man, on the other hand, was always struggling to pay his bills. Even so, he never set a fee for saving the city from a super villain.

Still, they desperately needed money. The pig story had hurt their business. Some long-time customers had stopped by to ask if it was true that La Chichen-Itza was killing pigs in the kitchen. Despite Rawly's mother's assurances that they weren't, many of those customers didn't return. But asking the Demetriuses for money? What would his mother say? "Hello, my son saved your daughter's life. You owe him a million bucks."

"Mom, I don't feel good about hitting the Demetrius family up for money," Rawly said.

"Let's not talk about that right now," she said. "It's late. You've got school tomorrow. Get ready for bed. And take your shoes with you."

Rawly was tired but not sleepy. He went to his bedroom and grabbed a stack of comic books from a box in his closet. He stretched across his bed on his stomach and thumbed through his comics. While he read, superhero catchphrases ran through his mind.

It's clobberin' time!

Avengers assemble!

Hulk smash!

Up, up, and away!

Rawly thought he ought to have a catchphrase, too. After all, he was a hero.

Grab it!

That's what he had shouted at Nikki before he pulled her out of the water.

Grab it! could work as a catchphrase. Okay, so it didn't have the same ring or excitement as *Flame on!* But then again, he didn't have super powers, like the Human Torch.

Rawly imagined carrying a billy club with an extension cable wire hidden inside it, like Daredevil. He would store it in a holster, strapped to his thigh. If someone was drowning, Rawly could whip out his billy club, press a button on it, release the cable wire and yell, "Grab it!" Then he'd pull the drowning victim out of the water.

Rawly would hang out at public pools, beaches and lakes, looking for signs of trouble. Lifeguards would have nothing on him.

Maybe he would have special T-shirts made with a picture of his billy club and the words *Grab it!* written across it. Sid Lundy could sell them at his store.

While Rawly was in the middle of an old *Superman* comic, he dozed off.

He dreamed he was back at Winnetka Creek. He could see Nikki Demetrius in the murky water drifting toward him. He dropped to his stomach on the bridge floor and dangled his shirt. "Grab it!" he shouted.

Nikki floated closer. Her skin was deathly pale. Her eyes were as red as her lips. Suddenly, she opened her mouth, revealing two rows of pointy, shark-like teeth. She lunged out of the water with her arms stretched and seized Rawly by the throat. His eyes widened with terror. He tried to scream, but his mouth only formed a silent O. He thrashed about the bridge floor, like a fish on dry land, trying to free himself from Nikki's powerful grasp.

Then he was yanked into the water.

Down, down, down, he sank. Rawly struggled to get free, but Nikki had her fingers locked around his throat.

Think like Batman! Think like Batman!

"Holy predicament, Batman!" he heard Robin's voice say in his mind.

Holy! That's it!

Rawly pulled out a small crucifix he wore around his neck. He tore it off its chain and pressed it against Nikki's forehead. The cross burned her skin with a steaming hiss, like a branding iron. Nikki shrieked savagely, then let Rawly go. She vanished into the darkness of the water.

Rawly quickly swam away. He cut through the thick folds of the creek water and sped to the top. He could see the sun's blurry image above. Faster! Faster!

As he was about to break through the surface, large tentacles wrapped themselves around his ankles and pulled him back down. He kicked at his feet, trying to free himself, but the tentacles continued to drag him deeper and deeper into the water.

Then Rawly woke up. His bed sheets were twisted around his legs. His room was dark, except for the red numbers on his digital clock and the subtle moonlight that seeped through his mini blinds.

Outside he heard the rain falling gently on the back porch and the gurgling water spilling from the down-spout of the rain gutter.

For the first time since the accident, Rawly realized how lucky he was that he hadn't fallen into the water try-ing to save Nikki Demetrius. His mother was right. He had taken a huge chance. If Nikki had pulled him off the bridge, he wouldn't have saved her. He wouldn't have been a hero. Nikki would have drowned. *He* would have drowned.

Shazzam!

CHAPTER TWENTY-ONE

When the bus pulled up in front of the school, Rawly wasn't surprised to see that Nevin wasn't waiting for him like he usually did.

Let him be mad. I don't need Nevin latching onto me. There are plenty of other people who want to hang out with me now.

Then, almost as if to confirm his thoughts, he heard someone shout, "Hey, Rawly! C'mere."

Cruz Vega was standing in front of the gym with a group of kids. A girl with short, reddish-brown hair had an arm wrapped around him.

Cruz announced to his friends, "This is Rawly Sánchez, the guy who saved that model's life."

"I saw you on TV," Cruz's latest girlfriend said. "You're kinda famous, aren't you?"

Rawly shrugged. "I guess."

"Rawly knows Jackhammer Jones from Channel 12," Cruz said. "And he's gonna get me an interview with him, aren't you?"

Rawly couldn't tell Cruz the truth now. He had dug himself too deeply in his lies. At the fair, Rawly told Cruz and his friends that he really had met Jeremiah Jones, and that Jackhammer (That's what he told me to call him) said how proud he was of him for what he had done. Jackhammer also said that if Rawly ever needed anything from him, all he had to do was ask.

By the time they met up with the girls, Rawly had gotten so wrapped up in his lies that he told them he had gotten phone calls from some of Hollywood's biggest celebrities, who wanted to thank him for saving Nikki's life. The only truthful part of his story was when he said that he was going to meet Nikki Demetrius in person.

Big Feo plopped a massive hand on Rawly's shoulder and said, "Cruz ain't the only star on the team, you know." Big Feo looked like a hippopotamus wearing a purple and white North Oak Cliff High School football jacket. The girl with him was a little smaller, a pygmy hippo. She wore an over-sized orange T-shirt and faded denim jeans. BOO! was written on the T-shirt in black letters. "I made five tackles in last Friday's game," Big Feo said. "You gonna get me an interview with Jackhammer Jones, too?"

"I'll try," Rawly lied.

"Hey, don't forget about my party," Cruz reminded him. "We're gonna have it at my cousin Frankie's apartment. He lives at the Vista Ridge Apartments on Tenth Street. You're gonna go, aren't you?"

Rawly smiled. "Sure, I guess. If I can get a ride."

"Don't worry about that," Cruz said. "You can go with me. We'll leave right after the game."

Rawly had attended only one game this season, when he and Nevin watched the Bisons defeat the Kiest Park Coyotes 24 to 14. His mother always made him work on Fridays, but Rawly didn't think he would have a problem getting Friday night off. How could his mother say no to her son, the hero?

"We'll order some pizzas," Cruz said. "And Frankie's getting the beer."

"Beer?" Rawly gulped. "But I'm not old enough to drink."

The group laughed.

"Tell you what, Rawly," Cruz said. "I'll get Frankie to buy you a Coke, okay? You can drink Cokes, can't you?"

The group laughed again.

Rawly turned red. He had said the wrong thing. He realized then that he didn't belong to Cruz's clique. He wasn't like them. He was out of their league.

Rawly began to have second thoughts about going to Cruz's victory party. It was one of those types of parties that had landed Jaime where he was.

The bell sounded

"I've got to go," Rawly said. "See you."

Cruz shook Rawly's hand. Then he reeled him in until their faces almost touched. "Don't forget about our deal," Cruz said. He smiled and released Rawly's hand.

Rawly left them, feeling shaky.

Arlie Hoyle and Santiago Pérez caught up with him.

"You know those guys?" Arlie asked in disbelief.

Rawly composed himself and said, "Sure. In fact, yesterday, me and Cruz went to the fair together."

"I don't believe it," Santiago said. "No offense, Rawly, but why would Cruz Vega want to hang out with you. I mean, you don't even play football."

"Ask him. He'll tell you." Rawly puffed his shoulders. "Cruz also invited me to a victory party he's having after the game Friday night."

"Now I know you're lying," Santiago said.

"Then don't believe me," Rawly said. "I don't care." He strutted off, trying to look important.

At lunchtime, Jennifer Barclay stood next to Rawly and asked Andrea Marino to take their picture with her camera phone. "You might turn out to be famous some day," Jennifer said, "and I want to be able to say I knew you when."

"He's already famous," Arlie said. "He's practically on every TV channel."

"Maybe they'll make a movie about him," Coy Deeter said. "I can see it now," he added, running his hand across the air, as if he was reading a marquee. "The Rawly Sánchez Story."

"Nah, it would need a cooler title than that," Arlie said. "More like, Rawly Sánchez, Teen Hero ."

"Yeah, that's a good one," Coy agreed. "That sound good to you, Rawly?"

Rawly didn't answer. He was watching Nevin, who was standing in the lunch line, being uncharacteristically quiet. Rawly thought about what he had done to him at the fair and felt bad about it. He wasn't ready to give up Nevin as a friend. He just wanted to teach him a lesson. As soon as Nevin got his food, Rawly would invite him to join him at his table. Maybe now that Nevin had learned what it felt like to be dumped, he would be a little more considerate in the future.

Rawly felt a pair of hands reach up from behind and cover his eyes. "Guess who?"

He couldn't mistake that voice. Rawly peeled off Miyoko's hands.

"Have you heard anything from Nikki yet?" Miyoko whispered in his ear. She had written down the names of the girls who were going with her to meet the fashion model, and except for Iris, no other girl at the table was on the list.

"Just from her rep," Rawly said in his normal speaking voice. "Nikki's still pretty banged up, and she wants to wait until . . . "

"Tell me later," Miyoko interrupted. She glanced around to see if anyone was listening.

"I saw your test paper hanging on the wall in Mr. Mondragón's classroom, Rawly," Iris said. "Looks like your algebra's improving."

"Thanks. I don't think I'll ever be great shakes at it, but I'm doing all right, I guess."

"Good," Iris said. "I told you, you could do it."

Nevin walked toward their table, holding his lunch tray. Rawly scooted in. There was an empty seat next to him. Nevin stopped. Ignoring everyone else, he leaned into Rawly and said softly, "A picture's worth a thousand words, my friend." Then he strode off and sat at a table across from them.

"What did he say?" Jennifer asked.

"I don't know," Arlie answered. "Something about a preacher's words. Maybe he heard something in church yesterday that's making him feel guilty."

"Nevin doesn't go to a church," Rawly said. "He's Jewish. He goes to a synagogue."

"Well, wherever he gets his religion, something's bothering him," Coy said. He nudged his head toward Nevin, who was hunched over the table, scarfing down his food. "What's the matter with your friend?"

"I don't know," Rawly answered. "He probably just wants to be alone."

"Maybe he wants to think about what the preacher said," Arlie mused.

Rawly knew what Nevin had said, and it didn't have anything to do with a preacher.

"A picture's worth a thousand words, my friend."

What did that mean? And why was Nevin sitting by himself looking sullen? Surely he couldn't still be mad about what had happened at the fair.

Aw, let him have his pity party. He's probably eaten up with jealousy because of all the attention I'm getting.

Perhaps it was time to drop Nevin as a friend. None of the other guys liked him. Whenever Arlie, Coy, Santiago or some of the other guys mentioned Nevin to Rawly, they sarcastically referred to him as *your friend.*

"Did you hear about what *your friend* did?"

"*Your friend* is an idiot."

Rawly looked around his table. *I've got plenty of friends. They're proud of me for being a hero. If Nevin can't handle the fact that I'm famous, well, too bad.*

Once again he shared with his friends the story of how he pulled Nikki Demetrius out of Winnetka Creek.

CHAPTER TWENTY-TWO

Rawly stopped by Heroes & Villains on the way to the restaurant. Sid Lundy had cut out *The Dallas Morning News* articles and had taped them to the window outside his store. A note on an index card was taped below the articles. It read: OAK CLIFF'S VERY OWN SUPERHERO, RAWLY SANCHEZ.

Sid was waiting on a woman who was arguing with her son, a boy in the fifth grade, who said he hated to read. The woman told Sid that she remembered reading *Archie* comics as a girl. She thought that if she could interest her son in the stories of Archie, Jughead, Veronica and Betty, he might develop a love for reading.

The boy refused to even look at an *Archie* comic, calling it a baby comic book for girls. He pointed to an issue of *Fangoria*, a horror magazine that specialized in slasher and splatter films. On the cover was a zombie with rotten teeth and decaying flesh.

"I'll read that one," the boy said.

"Not while you live under my roof," the woman answered sternly. She sat an *Archie*, an *Archie's Pal Jughead* and a *Betty and Veronica Digest* on the counter. The boy stood next to her with his arms crossed and his lower lip sticking out like a shelf.

"Ah, look who's here," Sid announced when Rawly entered the store.

Rawly waved at him.

"This is Rawly Sánchez, the young man who saved Nikki Demetrius's life the other day," Sid told the woman and her son. "I'm sure you read about him in the paper or saw him on TV. The articles are hanging on my window out front."

The boy's pouty expression disappeared, and his face brightened. "Really? You're him?"

"Sure am," Rawly said.

"Can I have your autograph?" the boy asked.

Rawly looked at Sid and the woman with uncertainty. "I . . . sure." He shoved his hands in his pockets to look for a pen or pencil. He brought them back out empty and asked the boy, "Do you have something for me to write with?"

Sid pulled a pen out of his shirt pocket and handed it to Rawly. "Here you go."

"What do you want me to autograph?" Rawly asked.

The boy picked up the *Archie* magazine from the counter. "Here. Sign this. Then it won't look like a baby comic 'cause it was autographed by a real hero."

Rawly felt weird being asked for his autograph, but he figured it came with his new role. He would have to get used to it. Now that he was a hero, he would probably be asked for his autograph all the time. He thought about writing a dedication line, but what could he say?

Of course!

"What's your name?"

"Stevie. Stevie Biggs."

Rawly signed the comic book: To Stevie Biggs—Grab it! Your friend, Rawly Sánchez.

The woman winked at Rawly and said, "I'm sure you love to read, don't you?"

Rawly understood her cue. If he was truthful, he would have answered, "Not really. Just comic books." But as a hero, he realized he was also a role model. It was part of his responsibility to say the right things. He handed the comic book to Stevie Biggs and said, "I read all the time. Reading makes you smart. You want to be smart, don't you?"

"Sure, I guess," Stevie said.

"Then read," Rawly told him. "Read a lot."

The woman winked at Rawly again. She said to her son, "See? That's what I've been trying to tell you. Reading makes you smart. And this young man should know. It took smart thinking for him to figure out how to save that girl."

Rawly had never been a role model before. It felt great.

After the woman and the boy left, Sid asked Rawly, "Where's your friend?"

Your friend.

"Nevin? Aw, he's a little mad at me right now."

"Oh?" Sid leaned on the counter and folded his arms.

"I think he's jealous," Rawly said smugly. "You know, now that I'm famous and everything."

Rawly had tried talking to Nevin again, but Nevin ignored him. He only repeated the words he had said earlier in the cafeteria: "A picture's worth a thousand words, my friend."

"Well, now that's the other side of being a hero, Rawly," Sid said. "People think it's all about fame and glory, but there's a lot more to it than that."

"Yeah? Like what?" Rawly asked.

Sid came around the counter and removed a Jimmy Olsen figure someone had hung in the wrong place and put it back with the Superman family of toys. "Heroes are held to a higher standard," he said. "They're expected to be kinder, nicer to everyone. If they're not, they'll be accused of being stuck up, of being arrogant." Sid stooped and picked up a gum wrapper from the floor and tossed it in the trash can. "Take that little boy whose comic book you autographed, for instance. You made his day. Being a hero isn't just about saving lives. It's also about being caring and treating others with respect."

Rawly furrowed his brows. Sid wasn't talking about that kid. He was talking about him and Nevin. *But I'm not stuck up. I care about others. I talk to everybody. It's Nevin who's mad at me because I abandoned him at the fair. But he had it coming. He deserved it. Like they say, people who live in glass houses shouldn't throw stones. Well, Nevin's thrown plenty of stones at me. If Nevin doesn't like it, then he shouldn't do it to other people.*

"Careful how you handle your fame, Rawly," Sid advised. "Folks can be fickle. One wrong move and they'll turn on you in an instant."

"I'll be fine, Sid. You don't have to worry about me." Rawly hurried down an aisle. He didn't need Sid preaching to him. Sid wasn't his father.

Rawly picked up the graphic novel *Watchmen* and thumbed through it.

Maybe Sid's right. I have been kind of rough on Nevin. I'll apologize to him for leaving him alone at the fair. Rawly smiled. *I'll tell Nevin I want us to be Jumex again.*

Nevin had a special quality Rawly admired. Most of the guys thought Nevin was an oddball, but that was only because they didn't understand that he functioned on a different level.

Nevin didn't listen to bubblegum pop music groups like the Jeremy Trio. He preferred the improvisational jazz tunes of Yells at Eels. You couldn't drag Nevin to see a chick flick like *Scarlet Dreams* or even the latest summer blockbuster. Nevin's taste in films was different from most fourteen-year-olds. Nevin once made Rawly sit and watch *Midnight Caravan,* a movie Nevin had rented, one that Rawly didn't understand until Nevin explained it to him. Nevin's quirky sense of humor often made Rawly groan, but he also had to admit that it was unique. There probably wasn't another kid at North Oak Cliff High School quite like Nevin Steinberg.

Besides, Rawly had bigger problems to deal with. What was he going to do about Cruz Vega? When was he going to tell him the truth? What would happen when he did? Twice, Rawly had seen Cruz in the hallways. Each time, Rawly had made a quick detour in the opposite direction.

Then there was Miyoko. Tomorrow he would be going to meet Nikki Demetrius, and neither Miyoko nor her friends would be joining him. How long was he going to keep stringing her along? Earlier, Miyoko had approached him and asked, once again, when they were going to see Nikki.

"Soon," he told her.

Miyoko read off a growing list of girls she planned to invite. "We can go in separate cars," she said. "Skye has her driver's license, so some of the girls can ride with her."

Why hadn't he just told her she couldn't go?

You know why. 'Cause you like her flirting with you, putting her hands all over you, that's why.

Funny how much Rawly's life had changed in a week. If he hadn't missed his exit that day, none of this would have happened. He would have gotten off the DART bus at the intersection of Zang and West Jefferson. He might have dropped by Heroes & Villains on the way to the restaurant to check out the new shipment of comics. Nikki Demetrius would probably have drowned, and Rawly might have read about her in the paper the next morning with little interest, since he didn't know who she was.

Cruz wouldn't have asked him to hang out with them at the fair. Rawly wouldn't have been invited to Cruz's victory party.

He would have just been the nerdy kid in the gorilla costume who had humiliated Miyoko Elena Chávez by squashing her guitar.

That night, Rawly dreamed he was back at Winnetka Creek. He was running along the bank, watching Nikki Demetrius floating in the water, thrashing her arms, screams gargling out of her mouth. Up ahead, he saw the bridge. He knew what to do. He had done it a million times before, in other dreams. Rawly ripped off his shirt and ran toward the bridge. Only this time, just before he reached it, he tripped on a rock and fell on his face, inches away from the bridge. He watched helplessly as the water currents carried Nikki away.

"Nooo!" Rawly jumped to his feet and ran after her, but it was too late. Nikki disappeared underwater and didn't resurface.

His dream switched to another scene, one of an ambulance parked on the street, its flashing lights shining brightly in the dark, cloudy day. Two paramedics were wheeling a gurney away from the creek. A body lying on the gurney was covered from head to foot with a white sheet. As the paramedics collapsed the gurney's wheeled frame to push it into the ambulance, the sheet caught on a side bar and was pulled down, exposing Nikki's ghostly face. She turned her head and stared at Rawly with wide, blank eyes.

"Why didn't you save me?" she asked in a cold, hoarse voice.

Rawly recoiled in horror. "I . . . I . . . " he started.

"You let me drown! You let me drownnn!" Her voice trailed off as she was wheeled into the ambulance.

Rawly woke up. He jumped out of bed and switched on the wall light. Perspiration beaded on his forehead, and his heart pounded madly.

He was no hero. It was by sheer luck that he had pulled Nikki Demetrius out of the water. He could just as easily have fallen into the creek with her.

Who knows? The currents may have swept her to the creek bank, where she could have crawled out of the water on her own. The Walmart worker and the girl had already called 9-1-1. The paramedics and the cop had shown up almost immediately.

Maybe his mother was right. He should have let them save her. After all, it was their job.

Rawly was still shaking from his nightmare, but he resisted the urge to go to his mother's room. He was four-teen years old, way too old to go crying to Mommy because he'd had a bad dream. Still, he wanted to talk to someone. He glanced at his digital clock. 2:36 it said. For a second, he considered calling Nevin. But it was the middle of the night. Also, he wasn't sure where he stood with him, not after the way Nevin had been snubbing him.

"A picture's worth a thousand words, my friend."

Rawly thought about his brother. If Jaime was still living at home with them, Rawly would have woken him up and told him about his nightmare. Jaime wouldn't have thought Rawly was a baby for being scared of a dream. He would have stayed up with him. They would chat until Rawly was so tired, he would fall asleep again. Rawly could always count on Jaime to comfort him.

Before his accident, Jaime seldom spent evenings at home. Their mother was usually working at the restaurant, and Rawly had grown accustomed to staying home alone.

Jaime would come in around ten-thirty, just before their mother did. Every once in a while, Rawly smelled alcohol on his brother's breath, but he never mentioned it.

The guys Jaime hung out with, Aaron Camacho, Jorge Bautista and the others were rough, thuggish types. Sometimes they would come home with Jaime. Rawly would hear them talking and laughing in the living room.

One night, a friend of Jaime's, a pimply-faced kid with blond highlights in his black hair named Eugene Castro, caught Rawly listening in on their conversation. He cussed Rawly out and told him to get lost.

Jaime scowled at Eugene. Then he calmly told Rawly to wait in his bedroom. A few minutes later, Jaime called Rawly back. Eugene had his head hung low. He apologized to Rawly for talking to him the way he did and promised never to do it again. Rawly never saw Eugene Castro after that.

Rawly didn't feel like getting back into bed for another dose of creepy dreams. Since he was awake, he decided to write to his brother. He still hadn't mailed him the newspaper article. Jaime would enjoy reading it. He would also get a kick out of seeing the Christopher Reeve/Rawly Sánchez double-panel picture.

A curious thought ran through Rawly's mind. Jaime had taken a woman's life, and he had saved a woman's life. Coincidence? Or was this God's way of evening things out? They say God works in mysterious ways. Maybe this was one of those mysterious ways. Rawly liked that idea. He thought Jaime might appreciate it, too. He decided to tell him about it in his letter.

CHAPTER TWENTY-THREE

Rawly was apprehensive but excited about meeting Nikki Demetrius. After the disturbing dreams he'd had, he wasn't sure what to expect when he met her. Also, his mother had been harping on him about asking the Demetriuses for money. This morning, they'd had a heated discussion over it.

"You let me handle things," his mother said when Rawly tried to make her promise not to mention money during their visit. "I'm a businesswoman and Mr. Demetrius is a businessman. He'll understand where we're coming from."

Rawly Googled Nikki's name. His mother was right. Nikki Demetrius had made a ton of money working as a model. According to her official Web site, she was born in Athens, Greece, the daughter of Andrei and Anastasia Demetrius. They moved to New York City when she was eleven months old. At age eight, she and her family moved to Dallas, where her father opened his first jewelry store. Nikki Demetrius was discovered a year later by Elaine Blaise, the founder of the Blaise Modeling Agency. Ms. Blaise noticed Nikki at Demetrius Jewelers, when she went in to buy a gift for her mother. Since then, Nikki had appeared in hundreds of magazine covers. She also had a fashion jewelry line of rings, necklaces, bracelets and earrings, which her father helped design.

The photos Rawly saw of Nikki Demetrius on her Web site and on television looked nothing like the disheveled, water-soaked, injured woman he had pulled out of the creek. He looked forward to meeting her now that she'd had time to recover from her ordeal.

Over the years, Rawly had met a few minor celebrities who dined at La Chichen-Itza. The cast of a low-budget horror movie called *Return to Darkness* had eaten there because they were filming nearby. But this would be the first time Rawly would be going inside a celebrity's home.

Out of curiosity, Rawly Googled his name. He was amazed by the number of news stories on the Internet about his rescue of Nikki Demetrius. Most of the articles referred to him as Rolando. A couple of others spelled his name Rollie, but Rawly didn't mind. He was thrilled to see his name on the Internet, regardless of how it was spelled.

The following day started normal enough. On the bus, the kids were pleasant, and Rawly chatted with his fellow riders. Once he arrived at school, things turned weird. Andrea Marino and Nicole Chadima, who had been friendly the day before, stared icily at him and walked away when he said hello to them.

In English class, Coy Deeter whispered something in Michelle McCutcheon's ear. Michelle made a face at Rawly and nodded.

What was going on?

After class, Coy told Rawly, "Don't let it go to your head . . . *hero*."

"Man, what an egomaniac," Santiago added, and both he and Coy walked off.

Rawly stared at them, bewildered. What was that all about? They had been friendly on the bus. Now they were avoiding him, as if he had the plague.

In science class, someone had erased the top of Rawly's head from the newspaper article that hung on the wall, and had enlarged it to twice its size. A caption read: Help! My head's swelling up!

Daniel Vásquez stopped by Rawly's desk and said, "What's your problem, man? You're not that big a deal."

"Watch it, Daniel," Travis McHenry said. "There's no telling how much Rawly will charge you for talking to him."

The guys laughed.

Rawly started to ask them what they meant, but Mr. Lazarski began calling roll. Rawly felt as if somehow, overnight, he had been transported to Bizarro World. In the *Superman* comics, Bizarro World was a planet called Htrae, Earth spelled backwards. The residents of Bizarro World did the reverse of people on Earth. Bizarro code stated: Us do opposite of all Earthly things. Us hate beauty. Us love ugliness. Is big crime to make anything perfect on Bizarro World!

The way the kids were acting toward him was the way a hero would be treated on Bizarro World.

While Rawly worked on an assignment about the interdependence and interrelationships of living things, Falesha Coe entered the science room and handed Mr. Lazarski a note.

Mr. Lazarski read it, then said, "Rawly, Mr. Hair would like to see you in his office right away."

Rawly looked up from his worksheet. "Why? What'd I do?"

Snickering broke out.

"I don't know," Mr. Lazarski said. "But I'm sure Mr. Hair does."

Rawly followed Falesha out the door. As they walked down the hallway he asked her, "Do you know what this is about?"

Falesha regarded him critically and said, "Maybe Mr. Hair wants to ask you for your autograph."

Rawly was confused by the tone in her voice. "Did I do something wrong?" he asked.

Falesha didn't answer. She picked up the pace and left Rawly behind.

Mr. Hair was waiting for him outside the main office. He greeted Rawly and shook his hand. "I enjoyed watching you on the *Today* show the other day," he said. "Good job. You handled yourself quite well in front of the cameras."

"Thank you, sir." Rawly didn't think he was in any trouble. But why did Mr. Hair pull him out of the middle of science class? Surely it wasn't to congratulate him for being on TV.

"You've become quite a celebrity here at school," Mr. Hair said. "I mean, it's not every day that one of our students fishes a famous model out of a creek." His voice tightened. "Still, we have policies and regulations that must be observed and obeyed. Being a celebrity does not entitle you special privileges."

"What do you mean, sir?" Rawly asked.

"Follow me." Mr. Hair marched down the hallway.

At the entrance to the library, flyers were taped on each of the glass double doors that read: BUY MY PHOTOS. $10.00 UNSIGNED. $15.00 AUTOGRAPHED.

Above the doorway was a photograph of the double-panel picture that had appeared in the newspaper. The photograph was printed on 8X10 high-gloss photo paper. It was autographed, Simply Super! Your friend, Rawly Sánchez.

Rawly gawked in disbelief.

Mr. Hair peeled off the flyers and the photo. "Now, Rawly, I know you're proud of what you did. I certainly am. But, son, you cannot sell these photographs in school."

"I didn't do that, sir!" Rawly insisted. "I've never even seen those flyers."

"These aren't the only ones." Mr. Hair pulled out a bunch of folded papers from his coat pocket. "I've been going up and down each hallway, on all three floors, taking flyers down from the lockers."

"I swear, Mr. Hair . . . " Rawly stopped when he realized his words rhymed.

"I have more of them sitting on my desk." Mr. Hair studied the photograph in his hand. "This picture is of a good quality, and I would hate to throw it away. You can have it back after school, but I don't want you selling your photographs on campus, you hear?"

"But I wasn't . . . "

"You can stand across the street and sell your photographs there, although I would discourage you from selling them at all. However, if I catch you selling them on campus again, there will be severe repercussions. Is that clear?"

"But sir, I didn't . . . "

"Is that clear!"

"Yes, sir."

"Good. Now go on back to class."

It didn't take Rawly long to figure out who was behind this. His suspicions were confirmed at lunchtime when he saw Nevin standing outside the cafeteria, waving a handful of photographs in the air.

"Photos of our hero!" Nevin announced. "Ten dollars or fifteen signed. Purchase either one, we really don't mind!"

Rawly stormed up to him. "What are you doing, man?"

"Hiya, hero. You wanted to be famous, didn't you? Well, I'm just helping you out." Nevin turned to the kids and pointed at Rawly. "Here he is, ladies and gentlemen. North Oak Cliff High's very own superhero, Rawly 'Good Golly' Sánchez!"

The kids gave Rawly dirty looks.

Nevin pulled out money from his pocket and slapped it in Rawly's hand. "Here you go, hero. I've sold three photos for you." He turned back to the crowd and continued chanting, "Photos of our hero! Ten dollars or fifteen signed. Purchase either one, we really don't mind!"

Travis McHenry sneered at Rawly and said, "Man, what a loser. Trying to make money off somebody's bad luck."

"But I'm not selling the photographs," Rawly told him.

"Of course you're not," Travis said. "You've got your idiot friend doing it for you."

Daniel Vásquez said, "I can't believe they found three kids dumb enough to buy those pictures." He chuckled. "Hey, Nevin, have you got any of Rawly in the gorilla costume sitting on Miyoko's guitar? I'll give you a dollar for that one."

"I'll look into it, my friend," Nevin said with a wink. "In the meantime, how'd you like one of these? I'll let you have it for five dollars. And since Rawly's here, he can autograph it for free. Right, hero?"

"I'm not signing anything," Rawly fumed.

Nevin shrugged. "Sorry, Daniel, no free autographs. Rawly wants his money."

"Give me those!" Rawly lunged for the photographs.

Nevin jumped back. "Nuh-uh! You'll have to pay for them like everyone else."

Rawly seized Nevin by the wrist and yanked the photographs out of his hand. As he pulled away, he accidentally smashed Nevin's nose with his elbow.

Nevin grimaced in pain and reached for his nose as blood trickled out of it.

Mr. Hair, who was on his way to the cafeteria, saw the commotion. "What's going on?"

Nevin began to bawl. He wiped his nose and smeared blood on his cheeks. "R-Rawly tried to make me buy one of his photographs, sir," he said in a frightened voice. "And when I refused, he . . . he punched me in the nose!"

Rawly's jaw fell open. "That's a lie, Mr. Hair! I wasn't selling the photographs. Nevin was."

"Oh, yeah?" Nevin blubbered. "Then why do you have the photos and the money in your hand?"

Mr. Hair gave Rawly a searing look. "Come on. You're going to the office!"

"But I didn't do anything," Rawly argued.

"Mr. Hair, can you call 9-1-1 for me?" Nevin whimpered. Blood had dripped down to his cream-colored polo shirt. "I need to go to the hospital."

The principal made a quick assessment of Nevin's condition. "I'm sure you'll be fine. But you'd better let the nurse take a look at you."

"I think my nose is broken," Nevin said. "If I had known Rawly was this violent, I would have given him all the money I had."

"You're such a liar!" Rawly screamed.

Nevin hid behind the principal. "Tell him to stop yelling at me, sir. He's scaring me."

Mr. Hair got in Rawly's face. "I've had just about enough out of you. Now settle down." He snatched the photographs and the money out of Rawly's hand and took the boys to his office.

As they walked down the hallway, Nevin smiled wickedly at Rawly and winked.

CHAPTER TWENTY-FOUR

Rawly got off the DART bus and made his way down Jefferson Boulevard. He groaned when he neared Heroes & Villains and saw his photograph taped to the window. He had been thrilled when he had first seen it on the Channel 12 News. Now the sight of the photo made his stomach turn.

Sid was standing behind the counter. He waved at Rawly and motioned for him to come inside, but Rawly ignored him and kept walking. He figured Sid was going to give him some more great advice on what it meant to be a hero.

Hero. Yeah, right.

Rawly was facing a three-day suspension for assault and for defying orders to stop selling photographs, even though he hadn't assaulted anyone or sold any photographs.

He had tried to explain to Mr. Hair what happened, but the principal found it difficult to believe that anyone would go to all the trouble to print quality photographs, sell them at school and give Rawly thirty dollars in profit, just to get revenge for being left alone at the fair.

"It doesn't make any sense," Mr. Hair told Rawly.

Of course it didn't make sense. It didn't make any sense to anyone, except to Nevin Steinberg. Nevin denied knowing anything about the flyers and the photographs when Mr. Hair asked him about them.

While Rawly sat in Mr. Hair's office, Nevin poked his head inside and threatened to sue the school if something wasn't done to control the "madman" who had beaten him up for no reason.

Mr. Hair didn't know Nevin personally, but he had heard stories about him from the teachers. There was an outside chance Rawly might be telling the truth, even if the truth defied logic. To play it safe, Mr. Hair wrote Rawly's mother a note, saying that she needed to come in for a conference. He would make a final decision then.

When Rawly arrived at the restaurant, the first thing he noticed was the newspaper article hanging on the wall next to the cash register. His mother had gotten it professionally matted and framed.

She was talking to a party of five. As soon as she saw him, she stretched out her arms and announced, "Here he is. My son, the hero."

The customers applauded.

Rawly's face reddened.

His mother introduced him to the people at the table.

A man stood and shook Rawly's hand. "I've never met a real hero before," he said.

"That's a real nice picture of you," a woman said, pointing in the direction of the cash register. "And what a great article. Congratulations, young man."

"Rawly, these people came to eat here today after hearing about you on the news," his mother told him.

"We've often passed by your restaurant, but we've never stopped in," the man said. "We thought we'd try it

today, hoping we might see the young man who saved
Nikki Demetrius's life. And here you are."

A nine-year-old girl handed Rawly her child's menu/
activity coloring sheet. "Can I have your autograph?"

Rawly sighed.

His mother pulled a pen from her blazer pocket and
gave it to him. "Go ahead," she said, smiling.

Rawly scribbled his name on the sheet of paper.

"Thank you," the little girl said. "I'm taking it to
school tomorrow to show my friends."

"Later this evening, we'll be going to the Demetriuses' mansion because they want to meet Rawly," Mrs.
Sánchez told the group.

They replied with *ooohs* of amazement.

"And I'll tell you what else," Mrs. Sánchez said, beam-
ing. "Rawly doesn't know this, but today he got a letter
from the mayor's office. The city wants to honor him for
his bravery. Can you believe that?"

The people applauded.

Rawly should have jumped with joy. His heart should
have burst with pride. This should have been great and
exciting news. But after what happened at school with
Nevin, after the way the kids had treated him, after the
way Mr. Hair had talked to him, he didn't want any more
recognition. He just wanted to put the whole incident
behind him.

He excused himself and went to the kitchen.

Fredo was standing behind the counter rolling enchi-
ladas. He looked up and said, "There he is, Super Rawly!"

"Did you save anybody else today?" Gerardo the dish-
washer asked.

"Maybe he saved a movie star this time," Enrique said. "Another person with *mucho dinero. Mucho, mucho dinero.*" He smiled, revealing his gold teeth.

Rawly didn't pay attention to them. He didn't feel like dealing with their jokes. He asked Fredo to fix him something to eat.

"Anything for the hero," Fredo said. "What would you like?"

"I guess I'll have the Tulúm Platter," Rawly said.

"An enchilada, a cheese taco, a beef fajita taco with rice and beans," Fredo recited. As he prepared Rawly's dish, an idea dawned on him. "You know what? We ought to change the name of the Tulúm Platter to the Rawly Platter."

"Yeah," Enrique agreed. "Or maybe the Hero's Special."

Rawly didn't say anything. He took his plate to the dining room and sat in a back booth. While he ate, he thought about his upcoming visit with Nikki Demetrius. He didn't feel like seeing her any more. Miyoko couldn't go with him, and he still hadn't told her. Miyoko was going to think he was a chump when she found out he had gone without her and her friends. What did it matter? Thanks to Nevin Steinberg, the whole school thought he was a chump.

Rawly fished Mr. Hair's note out of his pocket and read it. Sooner or later, he would have to show it to his mother. She had pitched a fit when she saw the failing notice. He wondered how she would react when she saw this. Rawly shoved the note back in his pocket. He would give it to his mother after their visit with the Demetriuses. Rawly finished his meal and went to work.

The restaurant was unusually crowded for a Thursday. Mrs. Sánchez took Rawly around to each table and

introduced him. A number of customers had seen him on
TV and said they were excited about meeting him in person. Each time, Rawly forced his lips to curl into a smile
as he retold his story.

After he shared his adventure for what seemed about
the thousandth time, he told his mother he didn't want to
talk to anyone else. He said he wasn't feeling well, which
wasn't entirely untrue. Rawly was sick of being a hero.

His mother told him to take a break. She wanted him
to be rested for their visit with Nikki Demetrius.

At six-thirty, a man named Bernard Jackson arrived
at the restaurant to pick Rawly and his mother up. Rawly
was disappointed when he saw that Bernard Jackson
wasn't driving a stretch limo but a green BMW sedan.

The three of them got in the car and drove off. It was
time to meet the Demetriuses.

CHAPTER TWENTY-FIVE

The BMW pulled up to a black iron fence. Bernard Jackson pressed a button on his remote control door opener, and the electronic gates swung apart. He drove his car around the circular driveway and stopped in front of the house. He stepped out of the car, opened the rear doors, and helped Rawly and his mother out.

Gazing up at the enormous, two-story brown brick home, Rawly blinked incredulously. Stately oak trees surrounding the house stood on magnificently manicured grounds. Between the gate and the circular drive was a large water fountain with a statue of the Greek goddess Aphrodite holding a pitcher. Water poured out of the pitcher and into the fountain.

Mr. Randall waited for them out front. He opened the door and led Rawly and his mother inside the house to the formal entry foyer, while Bernard Jackson drove the car to the garage.

A twenty-eight lights crystal chandelier hung from the ceiling. Across the room, dual marble staircases led to the upper level of the house. A grandfather clock standing against a wall startled Rawly when it began to chime. Rawly checked his watch. Seven o'clock. They were on time. He and his mother followed Mr. Randall to a spacious family room.

The first person Rawly noticed when they entered was Nikki Demetrius. She was seated on a brown leather chair. Her right leg, which was wrapped in an air cast, was propped up on the chair's matching ottoman. A bandage above her left eye hid her wound's stitches. Her right arm was supported by a sling. She was dressed in a white silk blouse and black cropped pants. Her hair was tied back in a ponytail, giving a full view of her face: high cheekbones, oval-shaped, dark-brown eyes and full lips. Despite her casual attire, Rawly thought she looked stunning. So different from the first time he saw her.

Nikki's mother, a dignified, slender woman, sat on a burgundy loveseat. Next to her was her twelve-year-old son, Michael. He still had on his school uniform—gray slacks, a white oxford shirt and a navy-blue sweater.

On the couch across from them sat Harold Skiles, an attorney, and Zane Archer, Nikki's publicist.

Mr. Demetrius, a barrel-chested man with black curly hair and a charcoal-gray suit that seemed too small for him, stood with an arm resting on the hand-carved mahogany mantle above the fireplace. Together they looked as if they were posing for a group portrait.

"Ladies and gentlemen," Mr. Randall said grandly, "may I present to you Mrs. Leonor Sánchez and her son, our young hero, Rawly."

Mr. Randall's introduction was met with enthusiastic applause.

"It is a pleasure to meet you both, especially you, Rawly," Mr. Demetrius said. He took Rawly's hand and shook it so hard it felt as if he was going to yank it off its socket. Everyone else, except for Nikki, stood and joined Mr. Demetrius in greeting Rawly and his mother.

"You'll excuse me if I don't get up," Nikki, said, "but it's a little hard for me to walk."

Daintily, she stretched out her hand. As Rawly took it in his, she pulled him toward her. She intended to kiss him on the cheek, but he moved his head, and her lips caught him on the mouth. It was the second time their lips had touched. This time, Rawly's toes curled up in his shoes.

"I owe you my life, Rawly," she said.

"We're all indebted to you, young man," Mr. Demetrius said. "We would have lost Nicolette if it wasn't for your courageous actions."

Still holding Rawly's hand, Nikki placed it lovingly against her face. "I don't know how I can ever repay you for saving me."

Mrs. Sánchez cleared her throat. "We can . . . discuss that later."

Rawly shot her a disapproving look.

Mr. Demetrius invited them to sit down. They discussed the accident, going over the details that Rawly had shared countless times. Rawly learned that Nikki had wanted to call him afterwards, to thank him, but Zane Archer advised her against it.

"I'm sorry, Rawly," Mr. Archer said. "But for days, Nikki was woozy from all the medication she was taking. I didn't think it was a good idea for her to talk to anyone until she felt better. You can understand that, can't you?"

"Sure," Rawly said.

Mrs. Sánchez told the group about her restaurant. She explained how difficult it was to keep it going during hard, economic times. "I'm doing my best, but with so little money coming in, I don't know how much longer I can keep it open," she lamented. She looked at Mr. Demetrius despairingly. He nodded but didn't comment on her situation.

Mrs. Carmona, the housekeeper, brought coffee and a tray of homemade chocolate chip cookies. She offered milk to Rawly and Michael.

While they enjoyed Mrs. Carmona's treats, Mr. Demetrius said, "Tell me, Rawly. What are your plans for college?"

He shrugged. "I haven't thought about it much. That's still a ways off."

Mr. Demetrius smiled jauntily. "It's never too early to start thinking about college, young man. Any ideas about where you'd like to go?"

Rawly shrugged again. "The University of Texas, maybe. That's where my mom wanted my brother to go before . . . " He caught himself.

"Jaime moved out of the house," Mrs. Sánchez quickly interjected. "He lives in a small town outside of Houston."

"I didn't realize you had other children," Mrs. Demetrius said.

Rawly's mother smiled awkwardly. "Just the two. We keep in close contact with Jaime, though. We try to see him almost every week."

Mr. Demetrius undid the button on his coat and released his ample belly. "The reason I mentioned college is that I'm setting up a trust fund to pay for Rawly's tuition to whatever university he chooses to attend." He turned to his attorney. "Harold?"

Harold Skiles retrieved a briefcase from the side of the couch and snapped it open. He drew out a form and presented it to Rawly and his mother. "While it is certainly our hope that Rawly will attend college, Mrs. Sánchez, the money will be his either way when he turns eighteen," Mr. Skiles explained.

Rawly's mother gave the paper a cursory inspection until she came across the monetary figure. She stared at it, saucer-eyed. It was more than enough to pay off every bill she had! Much more.

Mucho dinero. Mucho, mucho dinero.

"Can the money be used now?" she ventured to ask.

"I'm afraid not," Mr. Skiles said. "The trust fund is for Rawly's protection, Mrs. Sánchez. We want to ensure that the money will be there, if and when Rawly decides to go to college." He raised his index and pinky fingers while holding his middle and ring fingers down with his thumb. "Hook 'em, Horns!" he said. "I'm a UT grad myself. Good choice of schools, Rawly."

Mrs. Sánchez tried to hide her disappointment. She was grateful for Mr. Demetrius's generosity, but no one would be able to touch that money for another four years. At the rate things were going, La Chichen-Itza could be long-gone by then.

Standing alongside Nikki, Mr. Archer flashed a broad, publicist smile. "In the meantime, Rawly, we have big plans for you." He looked down at Nikki. "Shall I tell him or do you want to?"

"You go ahead, Zane," Nikki said. She winced as she readjusted herself in her chair. "It was your idea."

Mr. Archer checked to see if she was all right.

She nodded an *I'm okay.*

"We've kept up with all the stories about the accident, Rawly," Mr. Archer said. "And I must say, you made a terrific impression on TV. You were so poised, so confident, not a bit nervous in front of the camera." He rested a hand on Nikki's shoulder. "Here's what we have in mind. Once Nikki has completely recuperated, I want the two of you to go on a campaign together—on *Entertainment Tonight*, on *Access Hollywood*, on *E! Entertainment*, every celebrity gossip show on television." His eyes brimmed with excitement. "You have a certain look, Rawly. Slender, but not too thin, clear skin, not full of pimples, like a lot of boys your age. That blue shirt you used to pull Nikki out of the water. Where did you get it?"

"I don't know," Rawly said. "Penney's, probably. That's where we usually buy my clothes."

"Penney's . . . yes," Mr. Archer said, wrinkling his nose. "Well, we have a contract with the Christian Dior fashion clothing retailer. I suggested to Nikki that the two of you should appear in an ad together." Mr. Archer moved away from Nikki and gestured with his hands as he explained their plan. "This is just an idea, mind you, but one I think is worth considering. In the ad, Nikki would be in a waist-deep pool of water, with an arm reaching up. You would be lying on a bridge, dangling a blue, Christian Dior men's dress shirt above her. The ad would have a catchy slogan of some sort to go with it."

Grab it! Rawly thought, but he didn't offer it.

"We'll put out a full media blitz. The ad will appear all across the country. I think it'll be a huge marketing success." Mr. Archer grinned triumphantly.

"Would Rawly get paid for it?" Mrs. Sánchez asked.

"Oh, lord, yes," Mr. Archer said. "You don't think we do this for free, do you? Of course, all this is just an idea I want to pitch to the company. But we want to know what Rawly thinks."

Rawly would have cracked up laughing if he didn't know they were serious. Him? A model? That was the most ridiculous thing he'd ever heard.

Nikki sat up. "You don't have to give us an answer right away, Rawly. It'll still be awhile before I'm ready to go out in public."

"He'll do it!" Mrs. Sánchez said. "Rawly will make those TV appearances with you. He'll also be in that advertisement."

Rawly was speechless. He wasn't the model type. He wasn't even good-looking. If the kids at school were mad at him now, he couldn't begin to imagine what they would think if he started appearing with Nikki in ads. Earlier, Travis McHenry had accused him of trying to make money off someone's bad luck. It would surely seem like it now.

Nikki patted the overstuffed armrest on her chair. "Come sit next to me, Rawly."

Reluctantly, he got up from the couch and situated himself next to her. She wrapped an arm around his waist and asked the group, "Isn't Rawly awesome?"

They answered in agreement.

"You and I are going to be a team, Rawly," Nikki said. "After I get well, I'm going to show you off to the world. I want everyone to meet my hero." She ran her fingers against his back, shooting goose bumps up and down his spine. "I will take you to new places. You will meet new people. Everyone will know who you are."

"Yes! Yes!" Mrs. Sánchez chanted with a look of euphoria.

"Zane, I want pictures of Rawly and me in every newspaper in the country with the caption, The Hero and the Heiress," Nikki said. "This'll be our best campaign ever."

"We're going to make you a household name, Rawly," Mr. Archer said. "You're going to be famous. What do you think of that?"

Rawly was too stunned to reply. It had been fun, at first, seeing himself on TV and in the paper. He had enjoyed his time in the spotlight, being somewhat of a celebrity. But this heroing business was getting way out of control. He had no doubt that Nikki was grateful that he had rescued her. But she and Zane Archer were planning to exploit her accident, to exploit him, just like Miyoko. And Cruz Vega. And his mom. He looked over at her. She had her fingers locked together and was staring in a trance-like state. Rawly thought that if his mother was a cartoon character, she would have dollar signs in her eyeballs instead of pupils.

Mrs. Demetrius noticed the uncomfortable look in Rawly's face. To change the subject, she said, "Why don't we let Michael play a song for us?" She turned to her son. "If you don't mind."

Michael, who had taken piano lessons since he was five, made his way to the black Steinway grand piano and sat on the bench. "What do you want me to play?"

"What about *Clair de Lune* by Debussy?" Mrs. Demetrius suggested.

Michael opened his piano book and began to play the piece he had been learning from his piano teacher, Mrs. Curry.

Rawly scarcely heard Michael's song. His mind raced with thoughts of Nikki's plans. He didn't want to be on television with her. He didn't want to be a model. He didn't want to meet her friends.

He almost wished he had never pulled her out of the water. Not that he thought she should have drowned.

Someone else, Nevin perhaps, should have saved her. Nevin would know how to handle fame. If Rawly could, he would erase the past week out of his life.

When Michael finished playing, Mrs. Sánchez told Mr. Demetrius that they had to get back to the restaurant to help close up.

"You'll be hearing from us," Mr. Archer told Rawly and his mother.

Bernard Jackson brought the BMW to the front.

As they drove off, Mrs. Sánchez looked back at the house and said, "If things work out with what Nikki talked about, we could have a place like that someday."

Rawly didn't say anything. He was trying to figure out how he was going to live with himself after he let everyone down.

CHAPTER TWENTY-SIX

"You lied to me!"

Miyoko stormed up to Rawly with a newspaper clutched in her hand. Amanda, Skye, Melissa and Iris were with her.

Miyoko's eyes bulged out of their sockets and her nostrils flared. "Did you think I wasn't going to find out?" She waved the paper in his face. "You went to see Nikki last night, didn't you?"

Rawly took a couple of steps back. "Miyoko, I . . . "

"Don't try to deny it, Rawly!" she yelled. "There's a story in the paper that tells all about it."

Rawly expected Miyoko to be upset when she found out he had gone to see Nikki without her, but he didn't think she would be this mad. "Wait, let me explain. The thing is . . . "

"You promised we were all going to meet Nikki! I even asked you about it again yesterday and you said we were going soon."

"Miyoko, the fact is, Nikki didn't want anyone else seeing her, except for me and my mom," Rawly explained.

"Liar!" Miyoko's mouth contorted grotesquely. Rawly couldn't tell if she was smiling or baring her teeth, like an angry dog. "It also says in the paper that you're going to appear in an ad with her." Miyoko let out a strangled laugh. "Why would someone as famous and beautiful as Nikki Demetrius want to pose with a scrawny, horse-face loser like you?"

The girls laughed.

"You knew I wanted to talk to Nikki about modeling," Miyoko continued. "But you decided to steal my opportunity for yourself. Didn't you. Didn't you!"

"I don't want to be a model," Rawly said. "That was her idea, not mine."

"Well, in case you haven't looked in a mirror lately, I've got news for you, Rawly Sánchez," Miyoko said. "You're too ugly and too stupid to be a model."

Rawly had had enough. He could try to assure Miyoko that maybe once Nikki was ready to be seen by the public, he could arrange another visit, but he no longer cared what Miyoko thought. She had been using him all along, and her true feelings had finally come out. No matter what he did, in her eyes, he would always be a scrawny, horse-face loser.

"Look, I'm sorry, okay?" he shouted, not sounding sorry at all. "It just didn't work out, that's all."

"Yeah, you're sorry, all right," Miyoko said. Then she unleashed a stream of words Rawly didn't think existed in her vocabulary. He had never been cussed out in three languages before.

Miyoko stalked off with Amanda, Skye, and Melissa but Iris remained with Rawly.

"I really couldn't take anyone with me," Rawly told her. "Nikki's still pretty banged up from the accident, and she doesn't want anyone seeing her in her condition."

"I believe you, Rawly," Iris said, touching his arm. "But you could've told Miyoko. She was really excited about meeting Nikki. She told everyone it was going to be the greatest day in her life. She shouldn't have had to learn about your visit from the newspaper."

Rawly's face sank. He could handle being cussed out by Miyoko, but Iris's gentle reprimand burned deeper in his gut than Miyoko's ugly words.

"What about you?" he asked. "Aren't you mad at me for not taking you?"

Iris said, "I wasn't all that excited about going. I didn't even know who Nikki Demetrius was until Miyoko told me. Modeling's her thing, not mine."

When Rawly arrived at his first period class, he was met with cold stares left over from the day before. Luckily, he didn't stay in class long. The school was holding a pep rally to cheer the Bisons on as they prepared to play the Dallas North Bobcats, and all the classes were invited to attend.

The auditorium was packed. Rawly sat with some guys he didn't know. He hoped they wouldn't hassle him about the photos. He glanced across the room. Nevin was sitting next to Miyoko with a comforting arm around her. Rawly figured she was telling Nevin about the scrawny, horse-face loser who had lied to her. Nevin probably shared his story about how the loser had punched him in the nose because he wouldn't buy one of his photographs.

The band was seated onstage. They played the usual standards—theme songs from *Star Wars*, *Raiders of the Lost Ark* and Queen's *Another One Bites the Dust*. Rawly noticed Iris sitting in front of Mr. Gersch, the band director, playing her heart out on her clarinet.

What a contrast from her cousin. It was strange how two people from the same family could be so different. Iris had volunteered to help him with his algebra and hadn't asked for anything in return. Rawly realized that it wasn't just his confidence that had helped him improve his algebra grades. The strategies Iris had shown him worked. He had never even thanked her. He had pushed her away out of fear that the guys might think she was his girlfriend. So what was wrong with having Iris as a girlfriend? There were worse girls he could go out with. Rawly looked across at Miyoko and shuddered.

Cruz Vega and his teammates took the stage. After his usual bragging, Cruz spat out his annoying catchphrase: "We're on Cru-u-u-z control, baby! Woo!"

The cheerleaders jumped up and down ecstatically, as if the Bisons were playing the Dallas Cowboys instead of the 0 and 7 Dallas North Bobcats.

After the rally, Cruz and his friends caught up with Rawly. "Don't forget about my party tonight," Cruz said.

Rawly nodded but didn't say anything.

"You're still going, aren't you?" Cruz asked.

Rawly looked around the hallway. "I . . . I don't think I'm going to be able to go, after all," he said.

"Why not?" Cruz asked, sounding irritated.

"I've got to work tonight," Rawly said. "It's Friday and we're usually pretty busy on Fridays."

"Don't give me that," Cruz said. "The last time we ate at your restaurant was on a Friday night, and it was empty." His eyes bore down on Rawly. "You're not planning on backing out of our deal, are you?"

Rawly didn't answer.

"I'll bet you don't even know Jackhammer Jones, do you?" Cruz growled.

Rawly shrank back.

"You've been lying to me, haven't you, you little punk."

"Leave me alone!" Rawly watched in fear as Cruz and his friends circled around him.

"I don't like liars," Cruz said. "Especially punk, freshmen liars."

"You're the one who's gonna need a hero now," Big Feo threatened.

At that moment, Mr. Hair came around the corner. Cruz and his friends separated immediately, leaving Rawly quaking in near tears.

"What are you doing here?" Mr. Hair demanded.

"We were just talking, sir," Cruz answered right away.

"Not you. Him." Mr. Hair pointed at Rawly. "I told you, you weren't allowed back in school without your mother."

Cruz and his friends laughed.

"Poor baby," Eddie mocked. "Can't come to school without his mommy."

"Stay out of this, Eddie," Mr. Hair ordered. "Don't you boys need to be somewhere right now?"

"Yes, sir," Cruz said. He and his friends started off. Cruz turned around and told Mr. Hair, "Watch out for him, sir. That kid's a liar. He can't be trusted." The guys walked off laughing.

Mr. Hair crossed his arms and gave Rawly a smoldering look. "Did you give your mother my note?"

Rawly wiped his eyes with the end of his palm. "I didn't get a chance, sir. We were real busy last night and . . . "

"Let's go to the office," Mr. Hair ordered. "You can call your mother to come pick you up. You're being suspended for three days."

If there was a spark left in Rawly to urge him to speak up for himself, to try to convince Mr. Hair that he hadn't done anything wrong, it died out. So far, Rawly had been cussed out by Miyoko. He continued to be ignored by the kids, who just days ago had called him a hero. He had been threatened by Cruz, chewed out by Mr. Hair and now he was going to have to call his mother to tell her he had been suspended. And it wasn't even lunchtime yet.

The office clerk, Mrs. Miculka, pushed the counter phone toward Rawly. "Don't spend all day on it," she said. "This is a business phone, you know."

Rawly reached in his pocket. "I can call my mom on my cell phone."

"You use this one!" Mrs. Miculka barked. She returned to her computer and muttered something about kids and cell phones.

Rawly picked up the handset and punched in the numbers. "She's not answering," he said after a few seconds.

Mrs. Miculka looked up from her computer and rolled her eyes. "Well, try another number!"

Rawly punched the numbers again. "She's still not picking up." He was telling the clerk the truth. As long as he punched the phone number for time and temperature, his mother was not going to answer.

Mrs. Miculka threw her hands up in frustration. "What do you want me to do about it? Call her at work!"

Rawly tried again. The answer he got was similar to the last two: *The time now is ten-fourteen. Temperature, seventy-nine degrees.*

"She's not answering, ma'am," Rawly said. Then with a final plea he asked, "Can't I just stay in school for today? I promise I'll bring my mom on Monday."

Mrs. Miculka stared at him with disgusted resignation. "You wait here." She went into Mr. Hair's office. A moment later she came back out. She walked around the counter and motioned with a wagging finger for Rawly to follow her.

"Where are we going?" Rawly asked. For a moment, he thought Mrs. Miculka was going to throw him out of the building.

"In-house suspension. Mr. Hair doesn't want you in your classes until he hears from your mother."

Mrs. Miculka took Rawly outside to a decaying, portable building. Twelve boys and nine girls sat in the room working quietly. Mr. Geesler, a stout, elderly man with thick jowls and a strict face, better known by the kids as Mr. Geezer, was in charge of in-house suspension. He sat at his desk with his hands folded and eyed the trouble-makers.

This was Rawly's first trip to in-house suspension, so he wasn't familiar with the routine. "What am I supposed to do?" he asked.

"Sit down and be quiet," Mr. Geesler growled. "That's what you're supposed to do."

Rawly gazed around the room. A couple of the kids looked up at him with little interest, then returned to their work. "I mean, am I supposed to do some work or something?"

"Did you bring any?" Mr. Geesler asked.

"No."

"Then why in blazes are you asking me? Sit down and be quiet!"

Rawly picked the last seat in the row nearest the window and sat down. He had come empty-handed, so he had nothing to do. Rawly looked over at a boy in the next row and thought about asking him if he could borrow a pen and some paper. He could spend the time doodling. He decided against it when he saw Mr. Geesler's milky-blue eyes bearing down on him.

How long was he supposed to stay in here? Till the end of the day? Was he going to get to eat? Rawly looked around at his fellow inmates. He wondered what they had done to deserve being brought in here.

"I was caught skipping school."

"I was caught smoking in the bathroom."

"I was caught spraying graffiti on the walls."

"I'm innocent," Rawly would say. "I didn't do anything wrong."

"Yeah, right."

Rawly thought about Jaime. This was what it must be like sitting in a cell all day with nothing to do.

He wanted to see his brother, to talk to him. His mother was going to visit Jaime tomorrow. Rawly wondered if his suspension included Saturday school. Probably. If it did, then he would be free to see Jaime. On the other hand, if he told his mom he had been suspended, she might get so upset about it that she wouldn't take him with her.

Rawly looked at the bookcase across the room. It was mostly bare, but a few books were sitting on the shelves. He raised his hand. "Mr. Geesler, is it all right if I get a book?"

Mr. Geesler had his head bowed. He looked like he was either praying or sleeping.

"Sir?"

Mr. Geesler lifted his head and blinked several times. "Next time you come in here, you bring something to do," he said. "It's not my job to provide you with materials." With a flicker of his hand, he granted Rawly permission. Then he returned to his prayer or nap.

Three old dictionaries lay on the middle shelf. Rawly decided he would grab one if he didn't find anything else to read. There was a novel about the American Revolution on the upper shelf. That one might be interesting. Another book further down caught his eye. It was called *The Greatest Heroes of the Twentieth Century*.

Rawly pulled it off the shelf and took it back to his desk, along with a dictionary and the novel. He thumbed through *The Greatest Heroes of the Twentieth Century*. It was filled with short biographies of famous people, which included Mahatma Gandhi, Charles Lindbergh, Martin Luther King, Jr., Mother Teresa, César Chávez and a host of other great men and women.

Compared to them, Rawly was nothing. Those people had dedicated their lives to helping others. They had accomplished great things. Rawly had been lucky. He had been at the right place at the right time. Was he a hero? No way, no how. He would have to perform far greater deeds to earn that title.

That afternoon, when Rawly got home from school, he went to his bedroom. He tore the newspaper article off the cork bulletin board, wadded it up and tossed it into his waste basket.

CHAPTER TWENTY-SEVEN

On Saturday, Rawly still hadn't told his mother about his suspension. He did, however, manage to talk her into letting him go see Jaime. When she brought up the algebra failing notice, he reminded her that the notice didn't mean he was going to fail, and that his grades had gotten much better.

She didn't put up much of an argument because Rawly was right. His grades had improved. Besides, she was too elated at the possibility of her son being in an ad with Nikki Demetrius to criticize him for his school work. First he was a hero. Now he was going to be a star. His mother talked about it during the entire trip to Midway.

When they arrived at the Ferguson State Prison Farm, they went through the usual search routine before entering the contact room.

Rawly and his mother were shocked when they saw Jaime. He had a huge, purple knot on his right cheek. His left eye was blackened, and he had cut on his lip.

"*Dios mío*, what happened to you?" Mrs. Sánchez asked.

"Nothing, just a little accident," Jaime said. "It's okay, Ma."

"Who did this to you?" she demanded to know.

"Nobody. I, um, slipped on a wet floor."

"Did you report it to the guards?" his mother asked, not believing for a moment that her son had gotten that badly hurt from a wet floor.

Jaime looked around the room nervously. "Ma, it's okay. Really. I'm fine." To change the subject, he asked Rawly, "How are you 'manito? Long time no see."

"It was a last-minute decision," Rawly said. "Mom let me come because my algebra grades have gotten better."

"That's good to hear," Jaime said. "If I'd known you were coming, I'd have brought the surprise I've been working on for you."

"You mean the Torbellino comic book?" Rawly asked.

"I'm not going to say. If I told you, then it wouldn't be a surprise, would it?" Jaime said with a smile. "As soon as I finish it, I'll mail it to you."

"Did you get my letter?" Rawly asked.

"Yeah. I really enjoyed reading the article," Jaime said. "We were watching the news in the television room the day it happened. All of a sudden, they showed you pulling Nikki Demetrius out of the water. I jumped out of my chair and yelled, 'Hey, that's my little brother!' One of the guards told me to keep it down, but I said, 'That's Rawly. He's my kid brother. He saved that girl's life.' I don't think the guard believed me. None of the guys did. For a second, I almost didn't believe it myself. But it was you, 'manito."

"Did you see me on *Good Morning America*?" Rawly asked. "I was also on the *Today Show* and on Telemundo."

"Nah, we don't get to watch a lot of TV in here," Jaime said.

For a second, Rawly had forgotten where Jaime was. He looked around the contact room. This was probably the nicest part of the prison. Rawly couldn't imagine his brother living at the Ferguson State Prison Farm for the next fifteen to twenty years. Even if the lawyers did help get him out in seven, Jaime would never be the same. Not after having spent all that time in here.

Their mother told Jaime about their visit with the Demetrius family, about Rawly's scholarship, the television campaign Nikki and her publicist were planning, and of Rawly's chance to appear in a Christian Dior ad with Nikki.

"He's even going to be honored by the mayor for his bravery," she added.

Rawly sat in silence. He didn't know how he was going to tell his mother that he wasn't going to do any of those things. He wanted this whole hero business to be over with. At least it was making his brother happy. Jaime's eyes lit up as he listened to their mother.

"You've got a great future ahead of you, 'manito," Jaime said, his voice cracking. "Not like me. I sit here day after day, thinking about what my life could've been like if it hadn't been for . . . "

Mrs. Sánchez bumped Rawly's knee under the table. "Uh, let's not talk about that." Changing the subject she said, "The restaurant's been doing a lot better lately. Hasn't it, Rawly?"

This time Rawly didn't have to lie. Ever since he rescued Nikki Demetrius, people had been streaming into the restaurant. Some customers had come for a chance to meet him, but many others were returning a second and third time.

Jaime nodded. Then he said, "Ma, can I talk to Rawly alone for a minute?"

She eyed him curiously.

"Just brother-to-brother talk."

"Okay. I need to use the bathroom, anyway."

When she left, Jaime said, "'*Manito*, about what you wrote in your letter. You know, about how what you did was God's way of evening things out."

Rawly smiled. "Oh, yeah. Did you like that?"

Jaime's eyes narrowed with contempt. "Don't you ever think that, you hear me?" He spoke in a low voice so the guards wouldn't hear. "Nothing will ever make up for what I did. What am I supposed to tell that nurse's husband and their little girl? It's okay that I killed your wife, that I killed your mother, because my brother saved a woman's life, so we're even?"

That's not what Rawly had meant at all. He had written that part in his letter because he thought it would make Jaime happy.

"I killed a woman, Rawly!" Jaime's eyes watered up. "Don't you understand? I killed her! Nothing anybody says or does will ever change that. I'm already paying for what I did, so don't you dare talk to me about how God evened things out!"

Rawly had never seen his brother cry. Jaime had always been strong, tough. Nothing seemed to bother him. Even at the trial, Jaime had shown little emotion when the judged sentenced him to prison.

Now here he was, a Texas inmate, dressed in white, wrinkled, baggy scrubs. His hair looked like it had been clipped with hedge trimmers. His face was purple and black with bruises. And tears were running down his cheeks. Jaime didn't look tough any more. He looked sad. Pathetic.

Rawly came around the table and hugged him.

An inmate and his lawyer, who were sitting at the next table, stared at them briefly, then returned to their conversation. Rawly didn't care. He figured countless tears had been shed in the contact room over the years.

Jaime wiped his eyes and nose on his sleeve. "Don't be like me, 'manito. Keep making good grades. Work hard. Live a clean life. All that stuff Ma was talking about? Do it. And when you become famous, when I see you on TV, when I read about you in the newspapers, I'll be able to tell the guys in here, 'That's my brother.'"

When their visit was over and they were driving home, Rawly's mother asked, "What did you and Jaime talk about while I was gone?"

"Oh, guy stuff," Rawly said without elaborating.

"Guy stuff?" his mother asked, probing for more information.

When Jaime lived at home, he and Rawly used to share secrets they never told their mother. No need to change that now. There was one thing, though, that Rawly could tell his mother without feeling that he was betraying his brother's trust.

He looked at her and said proudly, "Jaime told me I was his hero."

CHAPTER TWENTY-EIGHT

That evening, while Rawly was bussing a table, Teresita called him to the phone.

He wiped his hands on a towel and headed to the counter, wondering who might be calling.

"Hello?"

"Hi, dude. You busy?"

Rawly hung up.

The phone rang again. He ignored it, but his mother rushed to the counter, frowning. "What's the matter with you, Rawly? Don't you hear the phone ringing?" Her voice changed to a sweet tone as soon as she picked up the receiver. "La Chichen-Itza Mexican Restaurant. How may I help you?" She listened for a few seconds. Then she said, "Yes, of course. He's right here. I hope everything is all right." She covered the mouthpiece and said, "It's Nevin. I think he's crying. You'd better take the call in the office."

Rawly sighed. He couldn't hang up on Nevin in front of his mother. That would require too much of an explanation.

He walked behind the counter, went inside the office, and shut the door. He picked up the phone and waited for his mother to hang up on the other line.

"What do you want, Steinberg?"

Nevin replied, "Something must be wrong with your phone, dude, 'cause I just called a moment ago and we got cut off."

"We didn't get cut off," Rawly said. "I hung up. Which I'm getting ready to do right now."

"Wait! Hear me out. Don't hang up."

Rawly paused.

"Please?"

"Say what you've got to say, Nevin, and hurry it up. I've got to get back to work."

In a halting voice, Nevin said, "I want to apologize for what I did to you in school."

Rawly sat in his mother's chair and waited for Nevin to continue.

"Dude, are you there?"

Rawly took a deep breath. A muscle twitched in his neck. "Why'd you do it, man? Why'd you make me look like an idiot in front of the whole school?"

Silence.

"Get lost, Nevin." Rawly started to hang up.

"Wait, dude! Don't hang up. I did it 'cause . . . I was scared."

Rawly put the phone back to his ear. "Scared? Of what?"

"Of losing your friendship."

That didn't make any sense. It was something Nevin was saying to get a reaction. It was part of his act, like pretending to be crying so his mother would put him on the phone.

"Well, you sure have a funny way of showing your friendship," Rawly said.

Nevin gulped. "Okay, dude. This is it. Confession time. I know this may be hard for you to believe, but you're the only friend I have."

Rawly knew it was true, but it sounded odd to hear Nevin admit it.

"So at the fair when I saw you taking off with those guys, I guess I sort of panicked. I thought I was losing you forever. I didn't mean to hurt you, Rawls, not really. I just wanted to get your attention. It was a dumb way of doing it, but . . . "

Rawly could hear Nevin breathing heavily. Then he heard him sniffle. It sounded as if Nevin really was crying. Nah. He was pretending again.

"Dude, you have it so easy," Nevin said. More sniffling. "You've got a ton of friends. Everybody likes you. They love hanging out with you, even old guys like Sid Lundy. But me? I'm nobody. I don't have anyone, except you. I can't even go out of the house by myself without my mom freaking out."

"But you always go out," Rawly said, not quite buying Nevin's story. "You go to my house, to the mall, to Heroes & Villains—"

"With you, dude. With you!"

There was no mistaking it. Nevin *was* crying. Rawly didn't know how much more crying he could take in one day. First it was Jaime, now Nevin.

"My mom doesn't think I can do anything right," Nevin said. "She treats me like I'm a baby. But she trusts you, dude. She lets me go out, only if she knows you're going with me. She's always throwing your name in my face. 'Why can't you be more like Rawly?' she says. 'He works. He's resourceful. He knows how to get around the city. It's always Rawly this and Rawly that. Now you're a big-shot hero." Nevin's voice rose to a high, whiny, level. "You couldn't even do something ordinary, like rescue a kitten stuck in a tree or help an old lady cross the street. No, you had to go and save a world-famous fashion model's life! You're on the news and everything. How am I supposed to compete with that?"

Nevin was bawling now. It wasn't an act, Rawly was certain of it.

"You have a cool mom who owns her own restaurant," Nevin went on, "but I'm stuck at home with the Paranoid Queen and Safari Bob." Nevin blew his nose. It sounded like a clown horn. "I've even tried to learn Spanish so I can be more like you." Nevin honked his nose again.

Rawly was surprised by Nevin's candid admission. He didn't realize Nevin regarded him so highly. Still, he was confused. How did Nevin expect to win back his friendship by embarrassing him at school with the flyers and photographs? He decided not to ask. Only Nevin's twisted logic could make sense of that.

"What do you say, dude? Can we be friends again? Can we be Jumex?"

Rawly knew the answer, but first he wanted to clear up some things. "I'll tell what would help," he said. "Try treating me like you really appreciate my friendship, all right? And stop acting like such a jerk."

"You're right," Nevin said. "I am a jerk. I'm a king-size, industrial-strength, restaurant-quality jerk."

Rawly wasn't finished. "You've also ruined my reputation at school. The kids think I'm a self-centered egomaniac. Plus, Mr. Hair suspended me for something I didn't do. What do you plan to do about that?"

"Hey, no problemo, dude," Nevin said, now sounding composed. "I'll turn myself in to Mr. No-Hair on Monday morning and confess my sins."

"What about the rest of the school?" Rawly asked. "How are you going to let everyone know that I didn't have anything to do with those photos?"

"Leave that to me," Nevin said. "I have my ways. I'll make sure your name is cleared."

Rawly was relieved. Sure, Nevin was a pain, but Rawly would much rather have him on his side than against it. "Hey, Nevin?"

"Yeah?"

"Glad you called."

"Me, too."

"See you at school tomorrow."

Nevin hung up. He flopped on his bed and propped up his head with a pillow. He folded his hands on his chest and gazed up at the ceiling.

"It's all about the sell," he said to himself and smiled.

CHAPTER TWENTY-NINE

On Monday morning, Nevin met Rawly when the bus pulled up in front of the school. Together they found Mr. Hair, who was monitoring the students on the blacktop. Nevin told the principal the truth about the photographs.

Mr. Hair apologized to Rawly for the misunderstanding. "To be honest with you, I didn't think you'd done it. I spoke with some of your teachers, and they seemed to agree with me." He shook Rawly's hand. "By the way, I received an email from the mayor's office, letting me know that the city wants to honor you for your heroism."

"He is a hero, sir," Nevin agreed. "Me? I'm a king-size, industrial-strength, restaurant-quality jerk."

"I'm not going to argue with you there, son," Mr. Hair said, winking at Rawly. "I'd like the mayor to present you with your award here at school, if that's all right."

Nevin grinned. "See there, dude. I told you I'd take care of things for you."

"Not so fast, Nevin," Mr. Hair said. "Starting tomorrow, you'll be spending the next three days in in-house suspension."

Nevin groaned. "But Mr. Hair, I told you what really happened, and I said I was sorry for what I did."

"I'm afraid that's not enough." Mr. Hair's face turned stony. "Do you realize how much trouble you caused for Rawly? For me? For the school? Playing practical jokes on people may be just a game for you, but sometimes there are consequences to pay. I'll make sure your teachers provide you with plenty of work to keep you busy."

Throughout the day, Nevin worked at convincing everyone that he, and not Rawly, was responsible for the photographs. Some kids, like Arlie, Santiago and Jennifer, accepted Nevin's explanation. Others, like Travis McHenry and Daniel Vásquez, told him to get lost.

Later that afternoon, Nevin found Rawly talking with Iris near the library. He bowed before her with one arm on his waist and other on his back. *"Hola, señorita. Perdón, pero tengo que hablo con Rawly."*

Iris sneered at him. "It's *hablar*, Nevin, not *hablo*. And I don't know why Rawly would want to speak to you. I can't believe what you did to him. You're supposed to be his friend."

Nevin reeled back. "But I am his friend."

"Not in my book," Iris said. "Why don't you grow up? Stop acting like such a clown. You don't impress anyone with your phony act."

Nevin's mouth fell open.

"If you're so starved for attention, why don't you try spending some time helping others?" Iris asked. "Earn the attention, Nevin. Don't beg for it."

Rawly tried to stifle a giggle, but it escaped anyway. *Get him, Iris.*

Iris squeezed Rawly's hand and said, "Call me, okay?"

Before heading out the door, she gave Nevin a parting shot: "Oh, and for your information, you're not nearly as funny or clever as you think you are."

Nevin stood rigid, as if he had been shot and was waiting to fall. Finally he said, "Man, she's starting to sound just like her bimbo cousin."

"Who? Miyoko?" Rawly asked.

"Yeah. I tried to explain to her about the photos and . . . Dude, she doesn't like you very much, does she?"

Rawly smiled. "No, I guess not."

"That's all right," Nevin said. "Consider yourself fortunate. That girl's about as bright as a flashlight with dead batteries—and just as useless. You know what, dude? If I ever do become Amnesia Man, Miyoko would be the perfect sidekick, Airhead. 'Cause if ever there was an airhead, it's her."

They made their way outside. Rawly froze when he saw who was at the bottom of the steps. "Let's go the other way," he told Nevin.

As he turned to go back inside the building, he heard a voice say, "Hey, Pancho! C'mere. I wanna talk to you."

Rawly stopped.

"Just so you'll know," Cruz Vega said, puffing himself up with self-importance. "Channel 32 covered our game Friday night, and their sports guy, Austin Spivey, interviewed me on TV 'cause I scored four touchdowns in the game against the Bobcats."

"And I made six tackles," Big Feo added. "Not that I care if you know about it."

"So I don't need to waste my time with a punk like you," Cruz said. "We're gonna have scouts from UT, Texas A&M and SMU at our next game."

"Big deal," Nevin said. "That doesn't mean they're going to offer you anything."

Cruz scowled at him. "Who's talking to you, nimrod?"

Nevin got in his face and said, "Beware of Greeks bearing gifts, my friend."

"What's that supposed to mean?" Cruz asked.

"You'll find out," Nevin said, smiling. "You'll find out."

Cruz and Big Feo walked off, with Cruz mumbling something about geeks and gifts.

As they watched them leave, Rawly said, "You know what, Nevin? Like it or not, Cruz is going to be a star football player someday."

"Why do you say that?" Nevin asked.

"Because he's a great quarterback. You heard him. He scored four touchdowns in their last game."

"Big whoop," Nevin said. "Al Bundy scored four touchdowns in a game, too, and he grew up to be a shoe salesman."

It took Rawly a moment to figure out that Nevin was talking about the character from the TV show, *Married With Children*.

"Come on," Nevin said. "Let's go buy some comic books."

CHAPTER THIRTY

A special assembly was held in the school auditorium to honor Rawly. The mayor and two city council members, as well as the school superintendent and three board members, joined Rawly and his mother onstage. Mr. Randall was also in attendance to speak on behalf of the Demetrius family. TV news cameras filmed the event.

The band was seated on the floor in front of the stage. They played the theme song from *Superman*. Iris looked up at Rawly and gave him a "thumbs up."

Mr. Hair addressed the crowded auditorium. He called Rawly's actions selfless and courageous. He said that he had never been more proud of anyone than he was of Rawly.

Both the mayor and the superintendent presented Rawly with plaques. In addition, the mayor awarded him the Key to the City, after declaring the day as "Rawly Sánchez Day."

Andrea Marino sang *Hero* while Nicole Chadima accompanied her on the piano. Rawly fought back tears as he listened to the lyrics.

Then a hero comes along with the strength to carry on, and you cast your fears aside and know you can survive. So when you feel like hope is gone, look inside you and be strong, and you finally see the truth that a hero lies in you.

When the assembly was over, members of the local and national news media interviewed Rawly, his mother, Mr. Hair and the invited dignitaries. They also asked students to comment on how they felt about Rawly. The reporters refused to talk to Nevin because he insisted on conducting the interviews wearing the gorilla mask, which he had taken to school for Halloween.

Rawly's mother had to rush back to work. The restaurant would be packed, and not just because it was Wednesday, and they were offering the enchilada dinner special. Business had boomed in the past couple of weeks. New customers were coming in every day. She gave Rawly the night off. He deserved it. She had asked Teresita's nephew, Arturo, who had been looking for a job, to come in and clean tables.

Since he was free for the evening, Rawly thought he might invite Nevin to go trick-or-treating with him. He decided against it. For one thing, Rawly didn't have a costume. For another, going door to door, wearing a mask, asking strangers for candy, now seemed like such a childish thing to do.

Perhaps it was time to put his trick-or-treating days behind him. He thought he might stop by the grocery store after school and pick up some bags of candy to hand out to the little kids who showed up at their door.

CHAPTER THIRTY-ONE

When Rawly arrived home, he checked the mailbox. It was stuffed with letters, bills and advertisements. One of the letters was from Zane Archer, Nikki Demetrius's publicist. Even though it was addressed to him, Rawly didn't open it. He would let his mother deal with it.

There was also a large manila envelope. He threw the mail on the coffee table and opened the envelope. Inside was a comic book, drawn on coarse, off-white paper. On the cover was a boy lying on his stomach on a bridge floor. He was dangling a blue shirt above a swollen creek. A woman, half-submerged in the water, was reaching up to grab the shirt.

The title of the comic book? THE HERO OF WINNETKA CREEK.